MISERABLE LOVE STORIES

25 *Romantic Disasters*
THAT ARE WORSE THAN YOURS

ALEX BERNSTEIN

Racehorse Publishing

Several of the pieces included here previously appeared in print or online at NewPopLit, The Big Jewel, The Legendary, Mid-American Fiction and Gone in 60 Seconds. Please rush right now to each of these sites and check out great works by much less depressing authors.

"The Bridesmaid's Dress," "The Brittany Clarke Interview" and "The 8-Hour Kiss" were first performed by None of the Above at the Westbeth Theatre in New York City. "Mother Pays a Visit" was first performed by Fantasy Shower Sequence at the Director's Club in New York City. "Back When" and "Toilet Paper & Kleenex" were first performed by Gi60 Next Gen at the Brooklyn College Department of Theater in Brooklyn, NY.

Racehorse Publishing books may be purchased in bulk at special discounts for sales promotion, corporate gifts, fund-raising, or educational purposes. Special editions can also be created to specifications. For details, contact the Special Sales Department, Skyhorse Publishing, 307 West 36th Street, 11th Floor, New York, NY 10018 or info@skyhorsepublishing.com.

Racehorse Publishing™ is a pending trademark of Skyhorse Publishing, Inc.®, a Delaware corporation.

Visit our website at www.skyhorsepublishing.com.

10 9 8 7 6 5 4 3 2 1

Library of Congress Cataloging-in-Publication Data is available on file.

Cover illustration credit: Getty Images
Interior art credit: iStockphoto/Getty Images

Print ISBN: 978-1-63158-583-8
E-Book ISBN: 978-1-63158-584-5

Printed in the United States of America

For Carolyn

Contents

MISERABLE
LOVE
STORIES

Clarity

I'M FALLING TOWARDS TRAIN TRACKS. SUBWAY TRACKS. THE F to be exact. It's about 9:20 pm. I'm falling towards the tracks because I've been massively sideswiped by a homeless man and his Samsonite luggage. It's a nice, sturdy suitcase—at least half the size of the homeless man himself. And sure, it's dingy, a bit blemished—especially near the bottom. But you really feel it when someone smacks it right into you.

As I fall, I notice that this is the second life-threatening transportation-related incident I've had in the last two weeks. And I wonder if it's coincidence or if I'm just not getting along with the New York byways. Perhaps the city's transit life-web is trying to tell me something— like—*get out of New York already, Bozo.*

The earlier accident had happened two weeks ago— the morning after I'd broken up with Daniela. As I was stumbling, depressed, across the street that morning I was run over by a bike messenger. The rider yelled at me: *I rang my bell, motherf–!* and sped off. Disoriented, I fell backwards, gashing my head on the metal crosswalk sign.

And as I lay on the ground bleeding, I realized that my problem was that I had hesitated. Not just with the bike, but with my entire life up to that point. My life, I realized, had been one long series of perpetual hesitations. Constant unwillingness to act whenever the time was right. I thought too much. Put my life on hold. Hesitated.

And realizing this, the moment became a moment of *utter clarity*. I needed, I realized, to make big changes in my life. Big big changes. And I knew—clearly—that the person I needed to make those changes with was *Julie*.

"Matt!"

"Julie!"

I had run into Julie the week before at the Greenmarket on 59th Street. Daniela was with me and, as always, was chipper, polite, and grating. Julie was with George, a doctor specializing in hair transplants, who had a real working microbrewery right there in his Manhattan apartment. *Just a hobby.* They looked oddly normal together—not yet in the love-hate-perpetual-fighting phase that Julie and I had once so greatly enjoyed.

And I smiled, made chit-chat, tried to be pleasant. I can't imagine I looked happy.

"George, this is Matt," said Julie.

"Matt-Matt?" asked George.

"Matt-Matt," said Julie.

"Some people triple it," I said. "Matt-Matt-Matt. Makes it easier to remember."

Julie smiled. George did a slow burn. Daniela stared at nearby melons.

Honestly, if not for the bike incident, I probably would've never seen Julie again. But now, *with clarity*, I decided to take action and call her. She agreed to meet me.

"Oh my God! What happened?!" said Julie, staring at the giant bandage on my forehead.

"You should sue!" she said. "Aren't there bike laws?"

"Yes," I said. "He didn't follow them."

We were at a little coffeehouse in Soho. We didn't talk about George or Daniela, the past or the future, or how we had left each other on extremely bitter terms. We kept things light. I didn't have much of a plan. We just talked, existed.

And it was nice.

Shopping at ABC Carpets with Kay, my life-long best friend:

"You can't seriously be thinking what you're thinking?" said Kay.

"What?"

"Getting back together with Julie."

"No—no—not at all—"

She stared at me, incredulously.

"You remember that awful girl you went out with Junior year?" said Kay.

"Amber? No—Terry—?"

"You were *so* angry with me! *With me!*"

"I know."

"You told me to never let you do that again! *Never!* You made me promise!"

"I know."

"We agreed to look out for each other!"

"I know—I know we did."

"Nine months! You were miserable, Matt! And you blamed me! Because I didn't talk you out of it!"

"I appreciate what you're saying," I said. "I shouldn't have blamed you. But this isn't like that."

"You wanted me to warn you. So here's your warning: *this is a bad idea.* A terrible, really bad idea. I know you and I know her. I even like her. I do. I think she has great, respectable qualities. But not for you."

We pass by beautiful red velour pillows. Soft and warm. They remind me of Julie.

"Maybe she'd like these," I say, picking them up, squeezing them.

Kay takes them from me, puts them back.

"When you and Julie were together you fought constantly. I've never seen a couple fight like you two fought. You were incredibly nasty to each other."

"I know."

"And one day you just walked out. Goodbye. Over."

"I know."

"And then what? Didn't her cat die?"

"Yes."

"And what did you say?"

"Kay—"

"What did you say?"

"I said—I'm sorry I just can't be there for you right now."

"Her fucking cat died!!!"

"Kay—"

"I mean—*holy shit, Matt!*"

"I know. *I know!* I was a big, miserable jerk! It was not a happy ending. Still—"

"It won't work."

"It might."

"It won't."

"It could. In a universe of infinite possibilities—hypothetically—it could work."

"It won't."

"I know this is hard to believe, Kay. But really, believe me. I know what I'm doing."

Says the man with a gash in his head falling towards the subway tracks.

As I fall, the irony of being sent to my death by a destitute man's suitcase doesn't escape me. But really, the bag seemed somehow inappropriate for him. It's cumbersome—can't be easy to lug up and down stairwells or get through turnstiles. Maybe it's more of a status thing. Maybe Samsonite elevates him to world traveler?

Two days after we met for coffee, I coaxed Julie into meeting me for a drink. Cautiously, I dangled the idea of us getting back together.

"Are you out of your fucking mind?!" said Julie.

So, Kay had pretty much nailed it.

"It's a shitty idea," said Julie. "An incredibly shitty idea. What were you thinking?"

"Well, actually—"

"I would never ever ever get back together with you, Matt. It's not just a bad idea—it's—it's upsetting."

"Then why did you meet me? Did you not think I wasn't thinking this?"

"I—I don't know what you were not thinking. I had no idea. I thought it was just a friendly, seasonal thing."

"Julie, you can't be happy with that guy. He takes undead hair scraps from people's armpits and buries them in their scalps! He makes beer in his living room! Is that what you want?"

"This has nothing to do with George."

And just like that it was old times all over again— arguing loudly in public places.

"Julie, when I was hit by that bike I had a moment of *utter clarity*—"

"I don't care about your clarity."

"—that *we should be together!* It was an epiphany."

"Your epiphany was wrong."

"It can't be wrong. It can't be right or wrong. It's an *epiphany!* It just is what it is. I'm not going to defend my epiphany!"

"Yours! *Your* epiphany! I had nothing!"

"Julie—"

"Where was your epiphany when my cat died?!"

"Julie—if I could go back—if I had a do-over—"

"A do-over!?"

"Look," I said. "I—I—it just—my point is—it just—it felt right. That's all. It made sense. It made sense to me. That's all I can say."

And she stared at me, tears welling up in her eyes.

"Why are you doing this to me?" she said. "You know how long it took to get over you?"

"I —"

"I don't trust you, Matt. And I will *never* trust you again."

I wanted to let it go. And I knew I ought to. But of course, I couldn't. I had conviction. She was upset, emotional. And I knew she didn't mean any of the things she was saying. I knew that after she had a chance to calm down and think about it, she'd know what she really wanted.

Or maybe it really *wasn't* the right thing? Maybe I didn't know what I was talking about. Maybe we weren't meant for each other. Of course, I knew if we got back together there would be yelling and screaming and fighting. But I didn't care about any of that. I wanted her despite all of that—because—because—in that moment of utter clarity what I knew was that

I WAS STILL IN LOVE WITH HER.

George couldn't make her happy. But me—in all my excruciating, miserable boorish crankiness, *I* would bring her joy.

So, I called. Unabashedly. Many times. I followed them to a few places. Stalked them, essentially. Left numerous unanswered messages. Her message to me remained clear: *Fuck off. Leave me alone.*

And Kay underscored that idea. Move on. Get on with your life.

So today, two weeks after my bike crash—at 9:15 pm—I had *new clarity*: I would let her go. Abandon my stalking.

For the last time I followed them down to the F train. The subway platform was bustling, and they saw me across the crowd. George looked like he wanted to slug me, but Julie held him back.

Our eyes met, and I knew it was over.

As I turned back towards the exit, I ever so gently grazed this homeless gentleman. And you know what happened next.

Now, in an effort not to appear overdramatic, I will tell you that no train was coming. But three things happened quickly:

- Time around me slowed;
- Julie yelled out: *Matt!* and
- I managed to swing my arm out, grab onto the nearby metal support beam and pull myself back onto the platform.

So, I never actually fell onto the tracks. I don't know why I didn't. But I didn't. The homeless man disappeared into the crowd, lugging his luggage behind him. The crowd on the platform gathered around me, concerned and generally freaked out. *Was I okay? Was I hurt?* Then Julie and George were there, too.

"Are you okay?" asked Julie.

"I—yeah—I'm fine—"

"I can't believe he just hit you like that! He could've killed you!"

"I'm fine, really—"

"Thank God!"

"He's okay," said George. "C'mon—"

"Stop it, George!" she snapped.

And they exchanged a look, signaling the sure, eventual heat-death of their relationship.

"You're okay?" she asked me again.

"I am. Really. I'm fine. Thanks."

She smiled, and took a breath.

"Take care of yourself, Matt," she said.

And they were gone.

And I came back up onto the street, feeling not so bad after all.

No, I didn't get Julie back.

But I'd gotten under her skin.

And I could live with that.

For now.

Barb

BARB WAS EXTREMELY POPULAR IN A WAY THAT I WAS extremely not.

There was something about Barb—the way she chewed her pens and threw them out before the ink exploded. And then I'd retrieve the pens and chew where she chewed, even if they did explode. And then I'd have blue teeth for weeks. And people would go, *Eugh. He's been chewing Barb's pens again. Loser!*

We had a special relationship, me and Barb.

She was always there for me. When I tripped in the hallway, she was there. When I spilled lunch on myself, she was there. When I got shoved into lockers, she was there, and usually helping to change the locks.

With Barb, the possibilities were limited.

On the *Charlie's Angels* Scale she was a 14.

Sitting near Barb was like sitting near a shampoo commercial.

Sitting near Barb was like sitting near a *Playboy* center-fold except she was real and alive and didn't have staples in her stomach. (That I knew of.)

Barb's third base was in four dimensions.

Barb was chick, perfected.

Barb's beauty was not only skin deep, but also blood, bone, muscle, nervous system, and organ deep.

With Barb, the world was not my oyster. The world was the oyster of the guys' over at the next table and they were not about to share despite their rampant shellfish allergies.

Barb's beauty was incalculable, unless you had a really good Texas Instruments calculator with extra log functions. (Which I had.)

Barb was out of my league. Actually, she was in my league. But she was a better hitter. While I closed my eyes and swung on every pitch.

Barb needed no cheerleading squad and could spell out "Go Team!" by herself.

Actually talking to Barb was inconceivable. The trick was to stand near her without melting.

Barb's beauty was so blinding I had to look through a pinhole in a cardboard box to see her (as if looking at an eclipse) which could be especially awkward in the school hallway.

Barb solved for Pi.

Barb was never full of baloney, cereal, or other animal by-products.

When God made Barb, he broke the mold. But a wandering hobo found the mold, glued it back together, and went to sell it to GE. But on the way over, he got hit by a school bus.

I would've worshipped the ground Barb walked on, but she walked on air. So, I worshipped air.

I only wanted Barb to validate me like a parking stub at jury duty.

We would have made the perfect couple, as Barb's grace and beauty would have offset my oafishness and malformation.

When Barb tried being a bad girl, society changed its perception of "bad" to "perfectly adorable."

Evenings, Barb worked at the broken lighthouse, guiding ships to shore with her smile.

Barb was a classic Greek beauty without the poor credit rating.

Barb's sweat was the universal solvent.

The sailor who gave up Brandy for the sea came back for Barb.

Barb not only conversed with woodland animals but also taught them French.

Barb didn't know I was alive, so therefore I wasn't.

Barb was proof that there was so much more that I could aspire to that I would never ever get.

Thinking back on Barb, I didn't realize how good I had it, back when I had it really good.

Had I had more courage, I would have surely told Barb how often I thought of her and how much she meant to me.

And she would have replied, "You're sitting on my coat."

The Bridesmaid's Dress

THE 1950S. SWEATER VESTS, BIKER JACKETS, BOUFFANT hairdos and greasy kid stuff. CYNTHIA (16) and TIP (16) her preppy boyfriend sit in a malt shop booth, holding hands and mooning over one another. Cynthia wears a large, hideous, bright, somewhat ragged bridesmaid's dress. The THEME SONG plays.

THEME SONG

Ever since the wedding,
She won't take it off!
Sure she spent some money,
But don't you ever scoff!
Did she lose her luggage?
Is she just obsessed?
Is her Mom a psycho,
who burned her clothes?
'Cause she only ever wears
the Bridesmaid's Dress!

Some SNOTTY GIRLS walk by and sneer at Cynthia.

GIRL 1: Nice dress!

CYNTHIA: Jealous!

They laugh and walk away.

TIP: Cynthia, before Dexter and Janet show up—
   can we discuss something?

CYNTHIA: Tip? What is it?

TIP: Gosh, the past few weeks have been so fast—
   we've hardly been apart—

CYNTHIA: It's been special for me, too, Tip.

TIP: Cynthia—I don't know how to say this, but I think
   it would be better if we took a break for a while.

CYNTHIA: (*shocked*) But I thought everything was
   going so well!

TIP: Oh sure! I just—

*An ELDERLY WOMAN walks by the table, and pauses,
noticing Cynthia's dress. She lifts the hem.*

WOMAN: I have these curtains.

The woman walks off. Tip grips Cynthia's hand, getting her attention.

CYNTHIA: It's my family!? They're too constricting!?

TIP: No—I love your family!

CYNTHIA: It's my hair—?!

TIP: I'm a big fan of your hair! All of it!

CYNTHIA: It's—it's—*MY DRESS!!??!*

TIP: NO! No, no! It's not the dress! It's—it's *me!* It's a personal thing, Cyn. I think we should just cool it down for a while.

Cynthia starts crying, loudly.

TIP: Hey, I'm just gonna go Jiffy-Lube my hair for a minute. Be right back!

Tip leaves. DEXTER, a jock, and JANET, a tough but nice chick, show up. They see Tip leaving and look confused. They sit with Cynthia.

JANET: Cyn! What's wrong?! Where's Tip going?

CYNTHIA: It's over, Janet. We broke up!

JANET: But why?

CYNTHIA: I don't know, Janet! I don't know!

JANET: Are you pregnant again?

CYNTHIA: No! It's not that! No one ever likes me after a couple dates! I just don't know why!

DEXTER: Maybe I better go have a little talk with the Tipper!

Dexter exits.

JANET: Now, listen, missy! You are not letting this get you grumpy! Come with me, Saturday—we'll go shopping.

CYNTHIA: For what?

JANET: You know—for—for—for—books!

CYNTHIA: I don't need books.

JANET: Fine chinaware!

CYNTHIA: I don't need chinaware.

JANET: New kinds of gum!

CYNTHIA: I don't need—

Cynthia stares at her. Janet is caught.

CYNTHIA: *WHAT'S WRONG WITH MY DRESS?!*
(*beat*) Are the sleeves coming off?!

She wrenches herself around trying to look at her back.

JANET: The sleeves are fine!

Cynthia is on the verge of bursting out crying again. FRANKIE, the coolest cat in town, comes over.

FRANKIE: Cynthia! Janet!

JANET/CYNTHIA: Frankie!!

Frankie sits, coolly.

FRANKIE: I see Tip broke up with you, Cyn! But that's okay!

CYNTHIA: It is?

FRANKIE: You bet! Hey! How'd you like to come to my pool party, Saturday? The gang'll be there! And I got a new tan that I'm itchin' to try out!

CYNTHIA: (*to herself*) *Swimming—swim suits—
flesh—revealed—*(*to Frankie*) Gee, I'd
like to, Frankie—but I just can't—

FRANKIE: No prob, slob! So then, after that, we're
all going mountain climbing! (*withdrawing
a large pick*) I got a new pick and I'm crazy
to stick it in a big 'ol hill! Come with?!

JANET: Eegah, Cyn! That sounds kooky!

CYNTHIA: (*to herself*) *Mountain climbing—
mountain gear—boots—parkas—*
(*to Frankie*) *I'm sorry, Frankie—I—
I can't—I—*

FRANKIE: Hey ho hey! Not a problemio! But then
after—we're all going to go strip down
and dress like babies! *Goo goo, gah gah
gah!* Hey! How's that sound?!

Cynthia convulses a bit.

CYNTHIA: NO! NO! I CAN'T DO IT! I CAN'T
DO IT! DON'T YOU UNDERSTAND?!

FRANKIE: (*stunned*) Wow. I mean—like—Wow! Uncool.

He gets up.

CYNTHIA: Frankie—Frankie—I'm sorry—I—

FRANKIE: (*coldly*) Well, you know what they say: "Always a Bridesmaid!"

Frankie leaves. Janet stares awkwardly at Cynthia.

CYNTHIA: (*shocked, stunned, etc.*) AAAAAAH!

JANET: Oh, Cyn! He didn't mean it!

CYNTHIA: Oh god! Oh god! I'm just gonna lock myself in a dark, damp, hidden bunker and no one will ever—

Dexter returns with Tip. Tip's head hangs low and he has a black eye.

DEXTER: I believe Mr. Tip has something he wants to say to Cyn, hon.

Janet and Dexter leave. Tip sits. Cynthia hurt, looks away from him.

TIP: Maybe—maybe I was jumping the gun,
Cyn—?

CYNTHIA: No—you're right, Tip. I've been thinking
and—I guess what I really want is someone
who accepts me—for me. For everything I
am. And for everything I wear. And I'm just
not sure you're that guy!

TIP: Gosh. Now who am I going to take to my
Aunt's wedding, Saturday?

He starts to get up. Cynthia perks up a bit.

CYNTHIA: *W-W-W-W-W-W-W-Wedding?!*

TIP: It's not a . . . big wedding.

CYNTHIA: I'm free Saturday, Tipper.

*Tip sits back down, excited. He takes Cynthia's hand. They
stare into each other's eyes again, gushing.*

TIP: Aw—who says you're inflexible, Cyn?!

CYNTHIA: I don't know! Who?!

They laugh and turn to the audience and freeze with gleeful smiles. The THEME SONG plays.

THEME SONG (Reprise)
Won't throw it out!
Won't take it off!

> *Maybe she just likes*
> *the Bridesmaid's Dress!*

Props

Vera's Journal
Friday, December 23, 1983
Newark Airport
9 pm

H ELLO. HELLO. HELLO.
I'm at the airport. I hate the airport. But you know that.

It's the most miserable time of the year.

My flight's not for another hour and forty-five minutes. It's unbelievably crowded—mostly with students flying standby, paying to get the cheap fares on People Express. The planes fly all night long and they're dirt cheap—you actually pay cash on the plane for your ticket—which is insane. What if you're on the plane and don't have enough cash? Do they send you back? Do they make you stow other people's luggage for four hours? Do they put you in the brig? *Do they have a brig?* These are the questions.

I can't stand the crowds. It looks and smells like a Grateful Dead concert. College students and teenagers attending prep schools (like me), trying to get home for the holidays. A sea of flannel and jeans. Kids have backpacks and sleeping bags. Some of them have unrolled their sleeping bags and are actually sleeping in them. I'm obviously avoiding the MOH girls. Six of them, in pajamas, are actually playing the *Mystery Date* board game on the floor at one of the gates. It's like a surreal summer camp inside the airport.

I decided to hole up at a gate with no outgoing flights just to get some extra space to myself. And I got bored quickly, so I unpacked my props and set them all up on the seats around me. And now it looks much more pleasant, if not a little fantastic. And why shouldn't it? If I'm going to be stuck here for hours, I might as well entertain myself. Besides, I'm so loaded down, I kind of like unpacking it all. A couple of *Mystery Date* girls already called me "Mrs. Claus" because the bag I was lugging was so huge. Yes, okay, it was probably stupid to bring all this stuff home. But if I had left them at school, they would have just gotten stolen like last year. And besides, I wanted to show Beth and my family some of this stuff. Not that they'll care. I had this great idea that some of my props might make great Christmas gifts. (Not to mention, they'll be collector's items after I'm rich and famous.) So, why not bring them home? I'm not 100 percent attached to *all* of them. I even thought I might leave a couple at the airport, so that they'd become "found art." My only worry was that some philistine would think they were garbage and throw them away.

For the record—since I know you're keeping a record—here's what I set out on the seats: a baby doll that's reversible and becomes a super creepy baby pig doll and a flag with bright red flamingos all over it (both from *Alice*); a huge, incredibly cool Coat of Many Colors (from *Joseph*, but it's really much more *Dr. Who, 4th Doctor*); a Rat Warrior, Nutcracker soldier, and a mini, plush, tie-dyed Santa (all from *Nutcracker*); Bondage Paddington Bear, covered in leather and metal studs (not from any specific show *yet*); a couple papier-mâché boulders (*Lost in Space!*); a pith helmet (no specific show); a couple other odds and ends; and of course, Buster.

I'm trying not to look at him directly, but there's an Indian kid sitting an aisle over who's been staring at me for like the past five minutes. He looks about my age—maybe a year or two younger. He's not even pretending not to stare. He's creeping me out, but I just unpacked all this crap, so I really don't want to move. He's wearing a bright blue prep school blazer. So, I assume he's from one of the academies. I've seen a lot of these kids wandering about. They're much more formal and don't go in for pajamas or sleeping bags like the Mary Olive-Harris (MOH) girls or the Deadheads. He looks pretty polished actually—except for the big hair. Wonder why they didn't make him cut it. He doesn't appear to have any bags. Just a cup of coffee he's been nursing and a paper that he's not even trying to pretend to read. *Creep.*

Or *maybe he's an exciting, mysterious stranger?!* But he's probably just a creep. I'm also creeped out by the homeless guy sleeping across two seats behind me who's snoring incredibly loudly. But I hate to move. I've got almost this whole gate area to myself.

9:30 pm

So, guess what? I actually started talking to the Indian kid!

First of all, his name is Bala. Bala Vijayan. (No idea if I'm spelling that correctly.) And he's only half-Indian. His father's from Bombay, but his mother's from Marin County. And he was doing the exact same thing I was doing—hiding from his classmates at an abandoned gate. I was right about the blazer, too. He's a ninth grader at McCarter

Academy in Westchester He hates crowds. The crowds here have made him extremely claustrophobic—and he saw me with all my stuff and thought I was doing performance art or a Christmas display or something—which would totally make sense if you didn't know me, right?

So, now I feel great that I pulled everything out of my bag. Even if it is a little freaky.

Which is what he first said to me, by the way:

"So, that's a little freaky."

"What is?" I said, pretending like I didn't know what he was talking about, but then admitting I did. Ha ha.

So then I explained how I'm the Prop Manager for the MOH theatre department and made these props for the shows this past semester. And that, of course, these aren't *all* the props I made. These were just the most significant and/or the easiest to bring home.

"You did a lot of shows in one semester," he said.

I really did!

10 pm

I found out more about Bala. (He's in the men's room right now.) He's been coming here, to Newark airport, as long as he's been at McCarter. Almost three years. I figured we must have been here at the same time at least a couple years, right?

His parents are divorced, and he hates them both, particularly his dad, who he spends Christmas with. But they don't get along at all. He said he spends so much time at the airport that he actually knows a lot of the people who work here on a first name basis. He knows Jesus, the guy at the Chock Full O' Nuts kiosk. (Bala drinks a lot of coffee.) He knows Millie at the Hudson Newsstand, and Paula the heavy Polish woman at Sbarro's. He doesn't like their food, but he likes Paula a lot. In fact, he actually prefers the airport to spending time with either of his parents.

He seems to have a lot of money. And, from what I can tell, his life kind of sucks. His father—who's a partner at a law firm in Boston—left Bala's mom for another woman. And now they already have an entirely new family together. Bala's dad had kids with this woman before he and Bala's mom even broke up. After that Bala got into so much trouble with drugs and stealing that his dad sent him to McCarter just to get him the hell away from the new family. Isn't that sad? You'd think he'd be more traumatized by all of that. But he seems pretty normal. (This, of course, coming from a girl who carts around a reversible baby pig and a talking plant.)

Oh. I freaked him out, by the way. I saw some woman throw out a perfectly good airplane sleep pillow. The big fluffy U-shaped kind that wraps around your neck that you can buy at the newsstand. I've always wanted one. Not just for the pillow, but because it's just so weirdly shaped and has so much personality, and it's gotta have like a million uses onstage. It could be like a tribble hotel, or a plush boomerang, or just a weird thing sitting on a dinner table. Pulling it out of the garbage almost made Bala throw up. But it was only in there a second and nothing touched it. I mean I'm not *that* gross. Oh! AND! The woman also threw out a sleep mask! *I've always wanted a sleep mask!* You can do anything with that, and it packs easily.

And Bala said, "if you want them so badly, why don't you just buy them?"

And I said, "of course I could buy them, but *the hunt* is everything. Finding these two things at once is a total jackpot!"

And he said, "what about diseases?"

And I said, "I've had enough experience haunting thrift stores to know when something's unhealthy. And these are a-okay."

And then he asked me who Buster is.

And I explained that Buster is my constant companion, my soulmate, and also a beautiful, stuffed, potted frond plant. He's my oldest and most favorite prop, and the first real one I ever created. Buster's been in every show I ever worked on. (He fades perfectly into the background.) We travel everywhere together. He's very lucky. And yes, sometimes I talk to him. What's it to ya?

"So, it's a security blanket?" he said.

"No," I said, "he's a close, non-judgmental piece of art, who knows me, intimately. And—since you didn't ask—he's named after Buster Keaton."

Bala didn't know who that was.

So, anyway, when Bala returns from the men's room, he said he's going to teach me how to play mancala. I already know how to play mancala, but I think it's cute that he wants to teach me, so I'm going to pretend I don't know how to play.

I think this is turning out to be much more of a fun airport story than I had expected it was going to be. Even if Bala is a bit snooty.

10:30 pm

News Update!

The planes here suck!

So, my flight got rescheduled to midnight. And Bala's flight got completely canceled.

We played like nine games of mancala—I beat him every time—and then he said why don't we go to the food court? So, we did. And everyone really does know him. The steak and fries guy, the Chinese food guy, that Sbarro's woman. They all knew his name and talked to him. It's surreal. They're giving him free food and the steak guy gave us free chef's hats. And we're still surrounded by all the thousands of students in jeans and pajamas, cause all of their flights are delayed, too. We pass the *Mystery Date* girls and they see us with our chef's hats on, and they're *so* jealous.

I got jerk chicken from the jerk chicken place which was pretty good. I thought it'd have bugs crawling around it—at Newark you expect bugs to be crawling on everything—but it was actually pretty good.

Then they called Bala's plane. So, we said goodbye and he left, and I was sad. He was actually kind of growing on me, y'know? So, I went back to my abandoned gate and started re-reading *Nurse on Terror Island*.

But then, ten minutes later, Bala was back.

"They canceled my flight," he said. "They haven't got another flight until two in the morning."

"That sucks," I said.

But I hate to admit that I was actually kind of thrilled. *More mancala!*

11:30 pm

I'm in the Delta Crown Room!

I made a joke about sneaking into the Crown room and Bala said, "I have a membership. We can go in any time. Want to go in?"

Duh! Yes!

He said he finds the Crown Room too snobby and quiet and prefers the main terminal crowd. But I am *lovin'* the Crown Room. It's a big lounge with attractive people and friendly waiters who treat you like royalty. And—and!—*Jackie O is in here! Jackie O!* She looks *great!* (For a—what—seventy-year-old?!) I thought she was talking to Eli Wallach for a moment—but I think it was just some other short, angry man. *But hey! Jackie O and I are in the same room together! I'm getting the same service as Jackie O!*

I'm suppressing a major urge to show Jackie my props. Jackie would *love* my props—especially *Bondage Paddington Bear* or my *reversible baby pig.* But I don't want to create a scene. Dammit. Next Time.

Bala told me he's never been to India, even though he has family in Bombay. (But his dad goes frequently for work.) Essentially, he's completely Americanized and has only the slightest Indian accent. And I realize I know *nothing* about India or Hindu culture. Nothing. And I feel so stupid. But he doesn't care. Just another stupid American.

I should get ready for my flight.

Midnight

My flight was delayed until 6:30 am tomorrow morning!

Holy crap.

So, I left the Crown Room to find a payphone to call my parents to tell them.

6:30?! What are you doing?! You can't stay there!

"I'm fine. I'm fine. It's perfectly safe. There's a million kids here whose flights are all delayed. In fact, I just met this one kid who—"

Why are you even talking to anyone?! Stay away from him! Airport kidnappings happen every day!

"No one," I said, "wants to kidnap me. Trust me."

But now they've got me all creeped out again. I'm not a kid. I'm 15. Assholes.

Wait. Okay.

That's bizarre.

I thought I just heard them call Bala's name over the PA system.

12:20 am

I got back from the payphone, but Bala wasn't in the Crown Room, so they wouldn't let me back in. At first, they acted like I imagined the whole thing—*no, he doesn't exist. He never existed.* But then they double checked and *yes, yes, he was here.* And they brought my prop bag back to me. Thank God. And Buster and everything else was still inside. And I asked if they knew where Bala went? Was he the one that they called on the intercom? They didn't know. They weren't paying attention. I realized I don't even know what airline he's on. People Express or Delta or God knows what. Something going to Boston, I guess. So, now I'm . . . kind of freaking out.

12:30 am

So, Bala was taken to a Delta security office!

Millie, the woman at the Hudson's newsstand, said she saw a Delta attendant escorting him through an "employees only" door to what was likely a security office.

Then she told me something that freaked me out more. She said she's pretty sure that Bala has been at the airport for a *couple days now.* She said she's definitely seen him here since Wednesday morning—because she'd left early on

Wednesday when she got a call that her kid was sick—and Bala had been in there talking to her when the school called—and that was definitely Wednesday. *Two days ago.*

So, then I ran over to Sbarro's and the woman there said, "Yeah, Wednesday seems right."

Jesus at Chock Full O' Nuts corroborated their story.

"At least Wednesday," he said.

"But," I said, "I just saw his flight get cancelled. I mean—that's what he told me."

"Well," said Jesus. "Maybe he had a lot of flights cancelled."

12:40 am

I knocked on the door to Delta security, but they wouldn't let me in.

But I could see Bala there in the back of the office.

I can't decide if I should help him or not. I mean—*he lied to me.* I should just let him rot.

12:42 am

Goddammit.

12:44 am

Shit.

12:46 am

Son of a bitch!

12:53 am

I just broke Bala out of the Delta security office.

We are now basically the *Bonnie & Clyde* of Newark Airport—if Bonnie was a pudgy fifteen-year-old girl with a bag of weird props and Clyde was a fourteen-year-old Indian boy with a mancala board and a huge mess of hair—and neither of them had guns. Jesus at Chock Full O' Nuts was instrumental in my Escape Plan. (And could have easily lost his job!) He brought a tray of hot coffee to the Delta security office and when the guy opened the door, Jesus "accidentally" spilled coffee all over him. C'mon! How *Starsky and Hutch* is that?! The attendant was furious and drenched. And when he ran out to the men's room to clean up—*I snuck in and freed Bala!* Then we ran down the airport midway to hide. After a couple minutes, they were calling his name over the PA system again—but then I got another great idea.

We went over to the remaining sea of Deadheady students (more like a small lake, now) still camped out in the People Express area and literally lied on the ground right next to them. Bala took off his academy blazer and put on my *Coat of Many Colors* while I put the tie-dyed, plush *mini Santa Claus* over us, and we were totally camouflaged!

So yes, sure, I had gotten Bala out of security, but I was still pretty incredibly pissed at him. And then he got real quiet. Which—y'know what?—is fine, because I have had it. I want nothing more to do with him. I helped him escape. That's it.

We are done.

6:30 am

Well.

So, it was a long, long night. Here's what happened next.

So, I sulked for a super long time, but by 1 am, I couldn't contain myself anymore.

"Have you really been here since Wednesday?"

"Yes," he admitted. "Early Wednesday morning."

"So, when you said your flight was cancelled—"

"I lied. I skipped my flight."

"Why?"

"I . . . don't know."

"How many flights have you skipped since Wednesday?"

"Uh—eight? Ten?"

"You made me think that that was the *only* flight you skipped!"

"I know."

"Why did you skip eight to ten flights?!"

"Because—I told you—I prefer the airport to going home."

"*That's insane.*"

"I'm aware of that. Nevertheless—"

"You can't stay here forever!"

"No, but you'd be surprised how long I'm capable of dragging out the inevitable. I have tremendous staying power. McCarter's been very good for that. Discipline."

"You dislike your father that much?"

"Dislike is a weak word."

"Why don't you talk to him about it?"

"I do. Of course. Nothing changes."

"He's going to be unbelievably pissed at you."

"Yes. That's why the longer I'm here, the less time with him."

A wave of anger washed over me.

"*I know families suck! Mine sucks, too! But they're supposed to suck, and you just deal with it!*"

"I'm sorry."

"*I trusted you.*"

"I know."

"*I liked you.*"

"I know. I like you, too."

Wait. Whoa. What?

"You—"

"I'm sorry I got you all caught up in my bullshit. I thought you looked like someone I could—I don't know—talk to. You seemed—interesting."

"Really?"

"Yes. In a weird way. With all your junk."

"Props."

"Right."

And then, at that moment, Delta security guards with dogs—*dogs!*—came by. So, we put our heads down. One of the dogs barked at a college student near us, who grabbed his bag and ran off down the midway. And the security dogs and guards chased after him.

We looked at each other, tired and exhausted, and we laid there for a few minutes and tried to play mancala. And we fell asleep.

"Hey! Hey! Both of you! Come on! Rise and shine! Let's go!" was the voice I woke up to at 5:30 am.

It was Bala's father, a gangly, older man with white hair and a very similar face to Bala's—but with anger lines etched into his forehead. He hauled Bala to his feet, forcefully. Bala, groggy and disoriented, put up little resistance.

"Hey!" I said, angrily. "Stop it!"

His father ignored me, so I yelled louder. *"Stop it!"*

"I'm sorry," he said. "Who the hell are you?"

"It doesn't matter who I am," I said. "He doesn't deserve to be treated like that."

"Doesn't deserve?" stammered the man, fuming. "Do you have *any* idea what I had to do to get here?! What I have to do *now* just to get him home?! *You have no idea!"*

"Well," I said, "if you weren't such an a-hole maybe he'd have gotten on that first plane Wednesday morning!"

He glared at me, furiously, then glared at Bala, and wrenched him up by the arm. Surprisingly, Bala resisted.

"Stop," said Bala.

"*People are waiting!*" shrieked his father. "*Do you know how fucked up this is!?*"

"And who's fault is that?" yelled Bala back at him.

I think Bala might have never yelled at his father before that moment. Now all of the student campers were awake and tired and grumpy, and they surrounded us. Bala's father looked at them, and me and Bala.

He took a breath and looked Bala in the eye.

"I know it's screwed up," he said, helplessly. "And I know it's my fault. But—I—am—trying. I am truly trying to make this right. Maybe you can't see that. But it's the truth."

He put a gentle hand on Bala's shoulder and spoke—what seemed to be—sincerely.

"I need your help, Bala," he said, "to try to make this year just a little less screwed up. Okay? Could you please try to do that for me? For once? For Christmas?"

Bala looked at me.

I nodded.

He looked at his father again.

"I can try to do that," he said.

"Good," said his father.

"But one thing," said Bala.

His father took a deep, worried breath.

"What?"

"This is Vera," said Bala, introducing me.

I grinned, stupidly. Bala's father glared at me.

"Vera's been here all night. And she may be in trouble now with Delta because of me."

"Fine," said Bala's father, annoyed. "Fine. Fine. Fine."

And so, that's why I'm now traveling on Delta first class back to Milwaukee!

Whoo hoo!

Bala's father, out of guilt—and also probably in an attempt to make peace with his son—upgraded my flight. And that's a-okay with me. I think it's the first time I've flown first class, actually. Almost as nice as the Crown Room! (Although no Jackie O.) I do feel a little bourgeois, like maybe I should be in the back with the losers and the proletariat. But hey! *I earned this!* Right?

So, I am considerably prop lighter now, by the way. I still had half an hour before takeoff and decided to see who was still on shift in the food court. I gave my *Coat of Many Colors* to a very excited Jesus. Paula was happy to get the *reversible pig baby*. And Millie was thrilled to get the *pith helmet* for her son. Bala requested the *tie-dyed Santa*. And I considered giving his father *Bondage Paddington Bear,* but I imagined that that would be a one-way trip to the circular toy box.

I've discovered that the neck pillow, by the way, makes an incredibly great—wait for it—*neck pillow!* (Although, it does smell a little garbagey.) And Buster is squeezed in right alongside me, here. Don't worry. He's not going anywhere.

So, that was my holiday airport adventure. Not what I planned when I started out. But hey, you go where life takes you. I think the best part is what Bala whispered to me as I left the gate:

"*See you, next year.*"

And that's a-okay with me.

Back When

*N*EW YORK CITY. THE EARLY 1900S, OUTSIDE A BROWN-STONE TOWNHOUSE. *WINTHROP* AND *CAMILLE,* *two teenagers, speak to one another.*

> WINTHROP: Camille—it was ever so pleasant to walk you home this afternoon.

> CAMILLE: Oh, Winthrop—it was marvelous. You're a true gentleman to carry my books.

> WINTHROP: Perhaps we might see more of one another?

> CAMILLE: That would be grand. Why don't you text me later?

> WINTHROP: Text you?

> CAMILLE: Yes, text me—or DM me. One of those things.

> WINTHROP: Yes, well here's the thing . . .

CAMILLE: Yes?

WINTHROP: You see, it's only the Year of our Lord 1913, right now—and well, there's just nothing to text you with.

CAMILLE: Nothing to text me with?

WINTHROP: I'm awfully sorry.

CAMILLE: Oh, that's fine. Then just Facetime me—

WINTHROP: Facetime you?

CAMILLE: Is that a problem?

WINTHROP: Well, you see it's that 1913 thing again. No texting, no Facetime. No Talky-Chatty boards of any kind, really.

CAMILLE: Nothing?

WINTHROP: No. I could send you a telegraph. But it would cost twelve thousand dollars and wouldn't arrive for two weeks.

CAMILLE: That seems inefficient. (*beat*) Look. Just come over at eight tonight and we can Netflix and chill!

WINTHROP: I almost don't know where to begin with that one.

CAMILLE: We can't do that either? Well, can we just watch regular television?

WINTHROP: *Nooo . . .*

CAMILLE: Go to a drive-in?

WINTHROP: Nope.

CAMILLE: Play MarioKart? *Please!?*

WINTHROP: Camille—

CAMILLE: Well, what *can* we do?!

WINTHROP: Take a lovely stroll around the park and enjoy each other's company!

CAMILLE: That sounds horribly dull. (*beat*) But . . . not so bad with *you*, Winthrop.

Cliffside

*J*ESUS CHRIST—WHERE THE FUCK AM *I*? IT'S—IT'S FREEZ-ING IN HERE. *Windy! Windy as shit! I'm—I'm—I'm—in a tent on a—I don't know—a raft?! A boat?! The thing is unsteady—no balance—keeps shifting! And the goddamn wind. Shit. I'm fucking freezing! Hung over. My brain is shit. I'm—oh God—I'm gonna—I'm gonna puke.*

What happened? There was—that girl. And now. Where's Dan? And is this even my tent? My tent wasn't this small. And why is it so goddamned windy?! No—no—we never even set up the tents! We weren't supposed to even get to the site till tomorrow! Shit—how bad was I last night? And—and what is all this constant swaying and shifting?!

Okay. Okay. Okay. I'm gonna stand—and—and—

I try to stand, but my slightest movement sets this little tent off-balance, like it's going to flip. My stomach's doing somersaults. I stay on my knees and edge slowly, slowly towards the front-end tent flap, trying to keep balance, but everything's pitch black and I have no sense of direction.

My shuddering, convulsing body is shaking the tent and then suddenly *all support gives out from under me! And I'm in freefall! Freefall! Falling swiftly through the blackness!*

Until I stop. Hard.

And then—then—I'm—I'm dangling—from some rope. Some noose or hitch-line. Now, the wind is whipping me, savagely. And I can hear my own voice—*screaming*.

I must stop panicking. Must—compose myself. I slowly fish for the mini flashlight in my lower leg pocket. Gingerly, I get it out, gripping it tightly. And I turn it on and see, finally, where I am:

Dangling off a sheer cliff.

A sheer cliff!

An almost dead man hanging in the middle of nowhere.

Her name was Melanie.

Dan and I had left yesterday evening. A guys' weekend to get away from the wives, families. We were going camping. And a few hours out, we stopped at a motel, dropped our bags, and went to the nearby roadhouse for dinner. It was almost midnight and the place was packed with bikers and locals.

"I think that blonde at the bar's got her eye on you," says Dan.

He was right. Curly-hair in pumps, jeans, and a flannel shirt. She smiled at me, sweetly. I made my way over to her, bought her a drink. She looked friendless and far away. But we connected and drank and danced. And a little while later, we were checking into a new room at the motel.

Half an hour later, she nestled, naked, under my arm. A perfect fit.

"You married?" she asked.

"Yeah," I said. "You?"

She held up a plain, small, perfect engagement ring.

"Got it yesterday," she said.

"Yesterday?"

She had gotten it from her longtime boyfriend. But clearly, she was already having second thoughts.

"He's a professional outdoorsman," she said. "He's that guy in magazines who takes tourists on paid overnight cliffside camping trips." But, she said, he was incredibly possessive of her. She'd already run away from him several times and he always caught up with her.

We fell asleep in each other's arms. A little while later, I awoke to her tugging on me, frantically.

"Hey!" she whispered. "You gotta get out of here!"

She shoved at me, aggressively.

Half-awake, I pulled my clothes on and scrambled for the door.

"*Go!*" she said.

I got just outside the door and then felt a violent crashing pain on the back of my head.

And the next thing I knew—*I was in the tent.*

Hanging by the rope, I sway violently, banging against the cliff. Below me: thousands of feet of nothing. My arms are scraped red. My ribs are on fire. But the merciless pain has cleared my head. *I'm alive*—so I *will* get back to the top. *I will find her—and I'll find that boyfriend that put me in that tent.* And when I do—

I'll kill him.

Twenty-five feet above me I see a flat, red rectangle dangling—the "bottom" of my tent. I pivot, but the goddamn rope is behind me, impossible to grip. I wrench back and forth, my chest burning. And I hear myself yelling:

I can do this! I can do this! You son-of-a-bitch!

Eventually, I get it—get hold of the rope and begin the long, brutal ascension. Pulling myself up is unending torture, but I take it inch by agonizing inch. What other choice do I have? My fingers are numb, and the wind is relentless. But forty-five minutes later, I'm back in the unsteady tent.

Progress.

Now, I'm wide awake. The peak is still several hundred feet up and my body's beyond dead—but anger and adrenalin fuel me onward.

Hours later, my hands ripped and bleeding from the climb, I reach the summit and collapse onto the first sturdy surface I've felt in forever. The euphoria is overwhelming.

"That's damn good time there, buddy," says a deep, craggy voice.

Standing over me is a gargantuan mountain man with ragged beard, cradling a steaming cup of something. He wears a large red parka. Nearby, I hear the engine of a truck.

"Yeah," he grins, "I'm the sumbitch that putcha in the port-a-ledge. That there's a freebie! Usually charge more 'n a grand for that."

"You tried to kill me!" I rasp. I want to grab at him, but my back isn't working the way it's supposed to.

"Shit," he chortles. "Wanted to kill ya, I'da just thrown ya off the cliff! Y'don't attach a goddamn safety line to some a-hole you're trying to kill."

I stare at him, hatefully.

"Would've come down for ya in another hour," he snorts. "But you were making such good time, I thought: what the hell!"

Then suddenly, this bear of a man hauls me to my feet and my body feels like it's going to rupture. He throws my arm over his shoulder and starts walking me to the truck.

"Where are you taking me?!"

"Back to your motel. Unless you'd rather walk."

"You left me down there!"

"I did indeed," he says.

I see the sign on his truck: CLIFF'S CLIFFSIDE CAMPING ADVENTURES!

"I'll sue the hell out of you!" I choke out. "You'll be in jail forever!"

He helps me into the passenger seat, buckles me in.

"Well, you could do that," he says, "and there'd prolly be a lot of media noise and yer wife and kids would hear the whole crazy thing. Young buck at a bar meets up with—"

"Stop! Stop it!" I say, helplessly, as he returns to the driver's side.

He looks at me and grins, gregariously.

"Coffee?" he says, offering me a cup.

I stare at him.

". . . sure," I say, defeated.

I take the coffee and we drive on.

He turns on a local country and western station and whistles tunelessly as he drives.

"She doesn't love you," I say.

"Maybe. Maybe not," he says. "Comes back a lot after some ugly nights with dudes like you."

"Like me?"

"Oh hell, you ain't the first guy got tossed in the port-a-ledge!"

And he laughs heartily all the way back to the motel.

Mother Pays a Visit

*J*EFF *AND* BETH *SETTLE COZILY ONTO THE COUCH WITH Chinese food and prepare to watch TV. Jeff glances over at Beth, and flirts with her. She flirts back.*

JEFF: I'm glad we got to spend more time together
      this weekend.

BETH: Me too. It's been great.

They watch TV. Jeff puts his arm around her. They look into each other's eyes, snuggle closer, as if about to kiss. Suddenly, a screeching, bird-like VOICE comes from offstage.

MOM *(OS)*: Jeff!? Jeff! Are you home?!

JEFF: Oh no.

BETH: Maybe if we're quiet, she'll go away . . . ?

MOM: Jeff?! Is that you? Are you here?! I love you!
      It's your mother, Jeff! Are you in there?

JEFF'S MOM enters in baggy housecoat and loaded down with several large suitcases. When she talks, she sounds like a broken, skipping record.

MOM: There you are! It's me, Jeff! Your mother! I love you! Who's this?! Who's this?!

JEFF: It's Beth, Mom. You've met, like, five times.

MOM: I'm his mother! I love him! Do you love him?

BETH: *(embarrassed)* Uhm . . . well . . . uh . . .

MOM: I love him! I'm his mother!

JEFF: I didn't know you were here, Mom.

MOM: I yelled! From outside!

JEFF: I guess I didn't hear you.

MOM: I yelled twenty-seven times! Since early this morning?

BETH: What did you say?

Jeff glares at Beth. She smiles, innocently.

MOM: "JEFF! THIS IS YOUR MOTHER! I LOVE YOU! THIS IS YOUR MOTHER!"

JEFF: Wow. I guess I just didn't hear you.

Mom suddenly withdraws a large knife out of one of her suitcases and threatens them with it.

MOM: YOU DIDN'T?! I COULD KILL YOU!

There is a short moment of intense fear.

MOM: Just kidding. I love him! I'm his mother!

She puts the knife away. They relax, slightly.

JEFF: Why don't you go upstairs and get some rest, Mom?

MOM: Oh no! I'll just stay here! I'll stay here with you!

BETH: *(to Jeff)* Maybe we could find her a hotel?

MOM: *(pulling out knife again)* Jeff! Jeff! I don't like her! I DON'T LIKE HER!

Another moment of intense fear.

MOM: Just kidding. Do you love him?

Beth grits her teeth.

BETH: Uhm—that's such a strong—

MOM: I love him, too!

BETH: You're his mother!

MOM: Right! That's me!

Suddenly, Mom drops all her suitcases, opens one up and starts rifling through it. She tosses clothes all over the room looking for whatever she is looking for.

MOM: Wait, wait, wait, wait, wait, wait, wait, wait, wait, wait, wait, wait, wait, wait, wait! It's here! I know it's here! I know it! I just know it's here! WAIT! Wait, wait, wait, wait, wait, wait! I know it's here! I know it's here!

She stops for a moment and looks up.

MOM: I'm his mother.

Mom dives back into her bags.

MOM: AH HAH!

Triumphantly, she pulls out a DVD.

MOM: *Deadpool!*

She puts it in the DVD player, nearby, turns it on, and sits down. She opens another suitcase, which is full of nothing but popcorn. She eats and watches TV.

BETH: I've never seen *Deadpool.*

MOM: Great movie! Stay and watch!

JEFF: *(to Beth)* Maybe we should go out?

MOM: STAY AND WATCH!

BETH: Why don't we stay and watch for a while?

They stay and watch. The movie comes on. After a moment, Mom leans over and talks to Jeff. He is annoyed by her talking during the movie.

MOM: How are you? You look well. Grampa bought a new car! It has a stick shift. I can't drive a stick shift!

JEFF: *(whispering)* Shh . . . not during the movie, Mom.

MOM: What's Bunco?! Everyone plays Bunco.

BETH: I think it's a game drunk Soccer Moms play.

MOM: Bunco! Bunco! Bunco!

JEFF: Don't encourage her.

MOM: When I was young, I had a kitten!

JEFF: Mom, please—

MOM: Her name was Snowball!

JEFF: Shhh . . .

MOM: Snowball got hit by a car! BAM! No more
      Snowball! Ha ha.

JEFF: MOM, SHUT UP!

Beat. Mom looks hurt. Like she may cry. Jeff looks apologetic.

JEFF: Sorry. I'm sorry. It's been a rough day.

*Mom smiles. They all sit back and watch the movie. Mom
starts singing.*

MOM: *Raindrops on roses and soft woolen mittens.*
        Flowers and laundry and two hundred kittens.
        Tie them all up with a big piece of string.
        These are a few of my favorite things.

She starts eating lots of popcorn while she sings.

MOM: *Basketball, horseshoes, and watching the Beaver.*
        Buying a new car and getting a fever.
        Pinching the waiter and having a fling.
        These are a few of my favorite—

Abruptly, she starts choking on popcorn. They watch her without helping. She chokes, falls to the ground, spazzes a bit—

MOM: Jeff! Jeff! I'm choking! I'm choking! I'm—
        Jeff! Jeff! This is your mother! I love you!
        I—I—I—

She chokes. Finally, Jeff smacks her on the back. She coughs out a piece of popcorn and passes out. They wait a second and then Jeff presses his fingers next to her throat, checking her pulse.

JEFF: . . . She's fine.

BETH: Want to finish the movie?

JEFF: Sure.

Pets

LIVING IN BROOKLYN WAS A LOT LIKE BEING MARRIED. Nick and I had already lived together for a year by then. So, after one more year in Brooklyn we were about as domestic as you get. We never talked about marriage because that was a subject that was forbidden, taboo. At twenty-two each, we both knew we were too young to even think about marriage. So instead, we tried to live life to its fullest and never uttered the M-word that seemed to hang so heavily over our apartment.

We had a lot of pets that second year. A dog, two cats and, ultimately, a tank of fish.

We both talked a lot about getting a dog. But what we really wanted was a cute, perfectly housebroken Cocker Spaniel puppy. However, the North Shore Animal League was all out of those. So, instead we got a mutt—some twenty-breed mix that no one could exactly identify. They thought he was probably a Labrador-Beagle mix with a hint of Terrier in there, but we guessed he was just a mutt, through and through. He was no puppy. He had at least a few years on him, and he certainly wasn't housebroken.

We named him Derby. Derby was a lot of fun for a few weeks. Then he was just exhausting. And Nick and I decided we didn't want the responsibility of having to take care of a poor dog in a small Brooklyn apartment when we both had to work long hours. So, we took him back to North Shore Animal League.

Then Nick said let's try a cat (because you don't have to take care of cats—they take care of themselves, which seemed much more in line with our lifestyle). So, I said sure, let's get a cat, and back we went to North Shore, because we were always intensely broke and their pets were free! This time, we got two cats: a golden tan one and a dark grey one. "Domestic longhairs" is what they were listed as, but let's face it, they were the cat versions of mutts. We named them Fritz and Felix.

Our new cats were extremely bored and sinister and shedding all the time. They shed absolutely everywhere, and I spent most evenings vacuuming cat hair off of everything. The tan one, Felix, used to perch on top of my stereo. I always forgot to put the dust cover over the turntable and he'd just sit up there on top of Elvis Costello's *Punch the Clock* and yawn and stretch and scratch away half of side one's tunes.

However, you couldn't hate the cats. I could. But you couldn't. Nick was right, I never really felt like they were *our* cats. I wanted something we could get more involved with and take care of, by ourselves. That was really *ours* to raise.

So, we bought fish.

We were very excited about the fish. We bought a $30 tank set with a four-gallon tank and a fluorescent light fixture and an air filter and colored gravel and a little sunken chest. We put it on a special table in the kitchen we bought just for our new aquarium. We bought all sorts of fish: red fish, blue fish, one fish, two fish, Neon tetras, goldfish and a catfish that would clamp itself up against the side of the tank and you couldn't tell if it was just cool like that—or dead. I think for a long time he was just cool and then, a bit later, dead, because at one point he just started rotting. But that was much later, after everything went green.

For the longest time we took really great care of those fish. I found the effect of watching them incredibly soothing. It was almost like watching tv, but more spiritual and holistic and centering. And, of course, no commercials.

The real drag to owning fish was that once a week we'd have to change the water. You'd have to take out all the fish and put them in some temporary fish-holding appliance, a pot or a vase or Ziploc Freezer bags that always accidentally started leaking everywhere, and then you'd empty the four-gallon tank, clean it out thoroughly, and then refill it. So, we'd do that every couple of weeks. Then every third week. Then every other month or so. Then . . . less than that.

So, the tank started to turn a deep shade of green and moss started to cover the top of the water. Nick told me he thought we might be cutting off their air, but I was pretty sure that all the stuff on top was algae and that they were eating it. So, now, instead of a fish tank, we had a small, organic pond in our kitchen. I was actually kind of proud of that in a way. We weren't even feeding them at this point. But they seemed to be doing pretty well for themselves, just living their lives (except that catfish).

And I got bored again and didn't want fish anymore. There was no motivation to take care of them. In fact, I realized, I was done with pets. I'd had it.

Soon, our lease ended, and we decided to move out of Brooklyn, and we knew that we had to get rid of all of the pets. Nick gave the cats to some friends. I flushed the fish. No remorse.

Shortly after that, Nick and I broke up. Our breaking up was a lot like a slingshot effect, where it was very intense near the end, then it just broke and it was over.

Right before the end, Nick admitted that he had thought about having kids with me. He had never thought about doing anything like that before, but he had thought about doing it with me. He liked the idea and thought I would've made a good parent. I was really touched by the thought. I beamed. For a moment, ignoring my relationships with the dog, cats and fish, I thought to myself, he's right.

I bet I would make a good mom.

The Brittany Clarke
Interview

*T*HE *TAWNY RUMAINE SHOW IN PROGRESS. TAWNY PLAYS*
host to famous actress BRITTANY CLARKE.

TAWNY: We're back! So. Brittany. Brittany Clarke!

BRIT: Yes.

TAWNY: This was it. This was the year that
Brittany Clarke took a second-rate
character—Joan Johnson—on the completely forgettable show, *Still Married!*,
which turned her into an *icon*.

BRIT: Well, it wasn't just me—

TAWNY: (*to audience*) Did she not revolutionize
television?! Yes! Yes, she did!

BRIT: Thanks, but you know in my new movie, I
play a very different—

TAWNY: Now. It was an issue before Joan, yes? But
let's face it—it was Tee-A-Boo.

BRIT: That's—that's right.

TAWNY: Whose idea was it? Who said—let's give
Joan Johnson *anal warts?*

BRIT: It—

TAWNY: Was that an idea?! Who said let's make an
entire year of plot revolve around Joan's
anal warts?!

BRIT: Not me.

TAWNY: No?

BRIT: Well, the show's a team effort. The producer,
Al Tandy. The writers, Jason, Phoebe and—

TAWNY: Your husband—

BRIT: Ex—

TAWNY: Ex-husband—Mandy Notrob! Wow! He
could see the impact warts would have on
the American mind! How did he know?
What made him think—Britty and warts?

BRIT: Well, we were fighting, actually.

TAWNY: Yes, you were!

BRIT: I'd become friends with—

TAWNY: Jerry Davici! Who wouldn't cheat on their husbands with Jerry Davici? I would!

BRIT: Yes, well, of course, Mandy found out. And the next day, Joan—

TAWNY: Had anal warts!

BRIT: Right.

TAWNY: Wow! So, you think he knew? That you and Joan and *Still Married!* would explode?! So to speak?

BRIT: Yes. I think that was his plan, actually. Hey—I brought a clip of my new—

TAWNY: Zwerdansk—a major pharmaceutical—asks Brittany to become spokesperson for their new product *Anal Wart Away.* But Britty says no!

BRIT: Well—

TAWNY: Millions of anal wart sufferers—women mostly—are now looking to you as a role model. Doesn't it make sense, then—

BRIT: Okay. Okay. Look. Let me just say, the last year
of *Still Married!* was one of the most exciting,
challenging years of my life. I can't tell you
how moved I was by all the love and support
from my fans. But—and I want to be clear
about this—*I do not have anal warts.* I'm a thin,
healthy, Hollywood actress who makes a living
playing a tired, bitchy, mid-western housewife—

TAWNY: With anal warts.

BRIT: *Had! Had* anal warts! We took care of it!
Remember?!

TAWNY: Of course! We were there with you all
the way, girl! Doctor's visits, wart inspec-
tions, scrapings and burnings, your
four-episode, thirty-six-hour surgery!

BRIT: Joan's free and clear, now! Just like me!

TAWNY: Now—you've just won your first Emmy.

BRIT: I did.

TAWNY: What a dress! Versace?

BRIT: Yes.

TAWNY: I noticed, in your acceptance speech . . .
you didn't mention warts.

BRIT: Look—

TAWNY: (*to audience*) Questions for Britty?!

A FRUMPY WOMAN in the audience stands and is handed a microphone.

FRUMPY WOMAN: Brittany, I've had anal warts for thirty years. But because of you, I'm not embarrassed anymore. Honey! Kids! It wasn't back trouble! It was warts! Big ones! With hair! Just like Brittany!

TAWNY: Such an inspiration you've been!

BRIT: Okay. Look—I know—each and every one of you has anal warts. I know you're proud of me and you all want to share. But I don't have warts! Or moles! Or boils! Or *fungusy* patches! Nothing! I have a perfect, perfectly healthy anus! And if I did have anal warts, I'd be so disgusted with myself, I'd probably blow my brains out!

TAWNY: Alright! Let's talk about that new movie!

BRIT: New movie? Right! Yes. Right.

TAWNY: *Baste and Murder!*

BRIT: Yes!

TAWNY: Which opens today in theatres across
the country—

BRIT: That's—that's right.

TAWNY: You play tough, leggy detective—
Maggie Anjowski—

BRIT: Yes. Right—a detective—

TAWNY: With anal warts!?

BRIT: No!

TAWNY: Did they get you special chairs?

BRIT: I—

TAWNY: With fluffy cushions?

BRIT: No! No! Look! Look! Wait—

Brittany stands, starts trying to remove her pants. Tawny grabs her. They struggle.

TAWNY: And that's all the time we have! We'll see
you tomorrow on *Tawny Rumaine!*

The Deli Chick

6 PM. SUNDAY. LATE DECEMBER. DRIFTWOOD PRICE CHOPPER. At the deli counter.

"Quarter pound of bologna, half a pound of Swiss. Finlandia," I say.

"Alpine Lace is better," says the Deli Chick.

"Yeah?"

"On sale, too."

"It's good?"

"Everyone says it's the best."

"I'll take half a pound."

"Honey ham's on sale, too. Boar's Head."

"Too oily. And he hates it."

"Try this."

She carves off a sliver. It's good. Nearby, Ryan, my eight-year-old, shoves a giant carving board into the cart.

"Ryan, put it back."

"It's bamboo. Hard bamboo. The whole thing!"

"We have, like, ten carving boards!"

"Really?" asks the Deli Chick, impressed. She chomps her gum like a roller-derby queen.

"No, not really," I say. "Maybe four. Of different sizes, though."

"The bamboo ones are better," she says. "Stronger."

"See?!" says Ryan.

"Better for the environment, too," she says.

"See?!" says Ryan.

"How's a regular carving board bad for the environment?" I ask.

"Well, forgetting the plastic ones, even the pine and oak ones wear out quickly. Whereas these are made out of—"

"Bamboo?"

"Which is a more plentiful resource, lasts five times as long, and is much easier to wash. Not that I'm saying you should get one . . ." *Chomp chomp.*

"See?" says Ryan.

"If you say 'see!' one more time, I'm going to put you through that meat grinder," I say.

"See see see see see see see see see see see," he says. "Put me through the meat grinder! Put me through the grinder!"

"Try this," she says to Ryan, handing him a frail, whispery piece of ham.

"What is it?"

"Ham," she says. "Try it."

He smells it, nibbles. His eyes bug out.

"You hate ham," I remind him.

"No, I don't."

"Half a pound," I say. "Skip the bamboo."

"Awww," they say in unison.

"Frankie! Frankie!" yells a kid in a tuque and Rutgers sweatshirt to the Deli Chick. He whispers in her ear and pulls something—tickets—out of his pocket. Her eyes widen, excitedly. Nearby, I pick through raw red hamburger meat. Ryan tugs on my coat.

"Dad—that guy in the hat's beating you out."

"Mm. Want meatloaf this week?"

"You better make your move!"

"Ah."

"Dad!" he pulls on my arm, staring back at the counter. "Now *another* guy's asking her out!"

"Let me know what happens," I say, moving on to poultry.

10:30 pm. Monday. Watching the Devils in my basement with Don, both of us in full Devils-watching gear.

"What about the one you met online?" says Don. "Melody?"

"Melanie. Very nice."

"And?"

"She looked good. A little tired. Couple years younger than me. Maybe forty-something."

"And?"

"Divorced."

"And?"

"Two kids."

"Professional?"

"Pharmaceutical something. Very nice. Very stable. Lots of charity work on the side. Volunteers with MS kids. Pretty big house."

"Sex?"

"Just met her, dude."

"So . . . ?"

"I dunno. She likes Bon Jovi. She went on and on about Bon Jovi. Bon Jovi, Bon Jovi, Bon Jovi."

"You don't like Bon Jovi?"

I stare at him.

"So, you're picky now?"

"I'm not into all this dot com stuff. Match.com. DriftwoodSingles.com. Jesus—I said I would never ever *ever* do this."

"Yer a fuckin' hermit."

"My grampa married once. When my grandmother died, he spent thirty-five years alone. And he was perfectly happy."

"So, being a shut-in runs in your family?"

"Exactly."

"No doubt he was getting it left and right."

"No doubt."

"Dude," he glares at me. "It's not good for you. And it's not good for Ryan when his number one role model is cranky and depressed all the time."

But I ignore him and watch the game.

9:30 pm. Wednesday. The Price Chopper parking lot.

It's freezing out. I'm bundled up, packing up the trunk. The lady in the car next to me packs up her trunk but her bag breaks and groceries spill out everywhere. Then, reaching to pick things up, she loses two more bags and everything's all over the place. I crouch down and help her, shove stuff in the trunk. And the wind whips around, fiercely.

"Thank you!" she yells.

"No problem!" I yell.

"I told him he was packing it too heavy!"

"Y'gotta pack your own bags!"

"He wouldn't let me!"

She pulls her scarf down, and—guess who? It's the Deli Chick.

"Hey! How's your son?"

"Good. Great. Home with a cold."

We're hopping back and forth, shivering.

"He's sweet!"

"Thank you. Yeah. I think that's all of it!"

"Thank you so much! What a nightmare!"

"Sure. Goodnight."

"G'nite!"

We head quickly to our cars. But I stop. I'm outside of my body—watching myself stopping, watching myself doing this utterly crazy thing.

"Hey—!"

She rolls down her window.

"I—I don't mean to be—to be—I don't know—creepy or weird or—"

"Uh?"

"Never mind. Never mind."

"What?"

"You wouldn't want to—I dunno—get a cup of coffee—with me—sometime?"

"Absolutely," she says. "How about now?"

"Now?"

"Or in an hour? I just need to put my groceries away."

"Oh—oh—okay. Sure. I'm Nick, by the way."

"Frankie," she says.

An hour later. In a booth at Leo Coffeehouse.

"My ex has a whole other family, now," I say. "Guy has two kids, two girls, and now they're having one together. It'll be Ryan's half-brother or sister or whatever. I don't even ask anymore, but it's fine. It is what it is."

"And he gets along with them all?"

"Yeah. When he sees them. Which isn't much. Sees them on the holidays. They're three hours away. Which is a little too close, a little too far—if you know what I mean. But the worst of it was over a couple years ago."

"Tough raising him yourself."

"Nah. My mom helps out. She's there now."

Her shoulders sink, relaxed.

"So, the deli, huh?" I ask.

"Yeah. The deli. I smell like meat all the time. And my feet and back are always killing me. But it's fine. Not quite what I planned to do."

"Does anyone plan to cut meat?"

"Oh yeah. The Deli Manager. He comes from a long line of—"

"Deli Managers?"

"Seriously. He does. Cutting meat's a whole family tradition with some people."

"But not you?"

"I got laid off six months ago and a girlfriend of mine told me they needed somebody a couple days—"

"And you're still there."

"And I'm still there. I don't like to brag, but I've put on, like, fifty pounds since I started."

"All that meat—?"

"Cheese. I'm a vegetarian."

"How can you work at a deli?"

"I'm not killing the fuckers. I'm just slicing and serving 'em."

She grins.

"I am so less hungry now," I say, smiling.

And she looks at me, looks into my eyes. And a little electricity goes off that I haven't felt in about ten years.

"Oh hey! There's one perk," she says. "The deli manager got me a work iPhone!"

She pulls out the latest iPhone. It's nicer and newer than mine, and I'm suddenly stupidly jealous.

"Kewl, huh? It's the latest model."

She leans closer to show it to me. And she does have a smell—a good smell—like meat and lavender. And the phone rings suddenly. And we both jump, surprised.

"My boss," she mouths, soundlessly.

"Yeah? Hello?" she says, answering.

"Deli emergency?" I say.

"Hey," she says. "Yes. Yeah, that works! Works fine. Uh huh. Okay. Great. No problem. Bye."

"All good?"

"Wanted to know if I could do the mid-day shift tomorrow."

"Can you?"

"Yes."

"Well, now I know why he got you an iPhone."

I stare at her, knowingly. She blushes.

"Please! He has kids!"

"If I was the Deli Manager, I'd get you three iPhones and a Vespa."

"Stop."

She puts it away, sees me glance at my watch.

"You have to go?"

"I—well—yeah, I should."

"This was nice."

"Yeah. It's nice seeing you, y'know, without a blood-stained apron on. Although, you wear it well."

She smiles, and then she's quiet, thinking.

"What?"

"I dunno. Nothing."

"What?"

"Well, I thought I'd ask if you—I dunno—you wanted to come back and smoke a joint with me or something."

"A joint?"

"Oh-my-God! Did I just say that? That sounded like a fifteen-year-old, didn't it?! I'm such a loser."

"No! Not at all."

"No?"

"No."

"So?"

An hour and a half later. Frankie's apartment. In bed.

Not how I had imagined the day would end.

"Nick," she says. "Can I be honest with you?"

Here it comes. I knew this was too good to be—

"I sneak pieces of meat."

"Oh. O-kay."

"What did you think I was going to say?"

"No idea."

She stares off, puzzled.

"I can't help it," she says. "I mean, some of the cold cuts are really good."

"They are good."

"I feel guilty recommending things to people if I haven't tried them, y'know?"

"So, you've tried everything?"

"Mm."

"Even the braunschweiger?"

"Yes."

"Y'know—you're an awful vegetarian?"

"I know."

I breathe easier, and I feel her warmth settle against me.

"You think we went too fast tonight?" she says.

"I—I dunno. What do you think?"

"Life's too short to be shy," she says.

10:00 pm. Thursday. Watching the Knicks in the basement with Don, both of us in full Knick regalia.

"She cuts meat?"

"Yeah. Short black hair, bangs. Always giving out free samples . . ."

"Wait-a-minute—! Chick with the nose ring?"

"Yeah."

"Dude—*she's hot!*"

"She's very nice."

"In one day?! You nailed the Deli Chick *in one day?!*"

"Well, that's being completely crass."

Don hugs me, forcefully.

"Dude! I'm effin' awestruck!"

"I think we were more on the same wavelength than I had originally thought."

"So?"

"So what?"

"So now what?"

"So now what what?"

"*So?*"

"So, I dunno. I just met her. She wants to take Ryan ice skating."

"*Bonding with the kid even!*"

"Yeah. He loves her."

Don stares at me a long time, then suddenly becomes cross-eyed, pained, angry.

"Oh shit. Screw you, man. Screw you!"

"What?"

"You've got a *but* in your eyes."

"I don't have a *but* in my eyes. I don't even know what that means. . . ."

"Dude—you totally have a *but* in your eyes. I know you! And this is where you always kill it!"

"I haven't even said anything!"

"You expressed *doubt*, dude!"

I stare at my half-empty beer.

"I dunno. It's just a little—sudden for me. She's like half my age!"

"You're what?"

"41."

"She's—?"

"28."

"That's a jackpot, dude! Let's call your ex and rub her nose in it—"

"Do what?"

"I'm kidding. Boy—look at you. Y'got all panicky for a second."

"Look, I think, in the rational, reasonable world, the world that Ryan and I currently inhabit—that the concept of *stability* isn't a bad thing."

"What?"

"Nothing. Forget it."

"Is she crazy? Unbalanced? Pissy?"

"No. Not that I know of, yet."

"She a heroin junkie?"

"No. She smokes a little pot."

"This is you in a nutshell, Nick. You freak yourself out too much."

"Yes, I do. I *do* freak out. Seriously. Sometimes, at night, I lie there, and I literally have anxiety attacks. What if something happens to me? What if I get hurt? What if I get killed?"

"What if you spontaneously combust? Like right now?"

"Right. Yes."

"Then we'd both be fucked."

"This is what I think about *all* the time. Yeah, I've got friends. I've got my mom. But it's basically just Ryan and me. The two of us—this micro-micro family. It's just too small."

He stares at me, at a loss suddenly for something clever to say.

"So maybe the Deli Chick is your road to stability?"

3:20 pm. Friday. Outside Driftwood Elementary.

Ryan bobs back and forth from leg to leg, looking anxious.

"Hey!" says Frankie. "Sorry!"

"I thought you forgot me—"

"No, no! I just—"

"I coulda been kidnapped like twenty times by now!"

"It's great that you weren't. So, you wanna go skating or what?"

7 pm. Friday. Front of my house. Frankie watches me shovel snow.

"I just—I couldn't get out," she says. "And I got stuck on the way over in all that fucking after school traffic."

"It's fine," I say. "Everything was fine. He had a great time. It's not a big deal."

"I was trying to race over and I'm honking at everyone and parking five blocks away. And he was really worried. I should've called you. I'm such a fucking idiot—"

"You could've called him. He has an iPhone too. For emergencies."

"Like his dad's stupid girlfriend being twenty minutes late?"

I stop shoveling and stare at her.

"So you're my stupid . . . girlfriend?"

She looks confused.

"Of course I'm your stupid girlfriend. Aren't I?"

I smile at her.

"Yeah."

10 am. Saturday. At the car wash, watching the shampoo shoot spray all over my Camry. Talking to Don on Bluetooth.

"I have absolutely no idea what I'm doing, Don. I need things predictable. Reliable. I completely made up my mind to end it. And now she's my girlfriend! It's *not* excellent! I was fucking furious with her! I mean—I mean—yes, I like spending time with her. I do."

I watch jets of water shoot freely all over my car, and roaring vacuums clearing every drop away in instants.

"I just feel so out of control, Don. And frankly, it scares me."

9:30 pm. Saturday. The Cactus Pear.

It's a little hole in the wall in the middle of Driftwood, barely room for a bar, much less the little sound stage for music acts. Frankie's dressed in jeans and a t-shirt. She looks great, hot, feral. It's open mic night and she's singing a couple songs to a small, but friendly crowd who seem to know her well. I stay in the back (if there is such a thing) by the bar, and watch. Me, the forty-one-year-old, invisible man. Two guys accompany her on guitar and a single snare drum. The drummer is tuque boy from Price Chopper. The other looks like his twin. Seattle grunge lives.

She starts with "Yellow Ledbetter" which seems more of a piece for her guitar player than her. But she delivers the unfathomable lyrics with a deep, husky, guttural sound. She follows with a screeching "Piece of my Heart" that surprises me, and closes with a slow, slow song that I haven't heard in years, and that, for a moment, is even smokier than Janis.

> *Come to me, my melancholy baby,*
> *Cuddle up and don't be blue.*
> *All your fears are foolish fancy, maybe,*
> *You know dear,*
> *that I am strong for you.*

And she's like some beautiful, ethereal creature— pained, wounded, fragile. My heart beats faster as I hear the ache behind her words. *Am I doing this to her? Are we doing this to each other?* Drenched with sweat, hair matted, she finishes. The crowd hoots, hollers, and I'm right there with them.

2:30 am. Her place.

I wake up, suddenly, see the clock and panic.

"Shit! I fell asleep!"

"Your mother—"

"Babysitter! Got a babysitter! Shit! Shit! I gotta go!"

2:40 am. Home.

Sixteen-year-old Laurie is asleep on the couch. Next to her, wide awake and pissed, is her mother.

"I am so sorry," I say. "I—I—I—there was an accident and—"

I'm an incredibly awful liar. But it doesn't matter. The mom, disgusted, tugs at her daughter.

"Laurie—Laurie—let's go. C'mon."

And they leave. The house is silent.

7 pm. Sunday. Driftwood Café.

Frankie and I have coffee. We say nothing. She stares away from me, out the window, hurt, angry. I feel like shit. She gets up, and walks out, and doesn't look back.

9 pm. The upstairs hallway outside the bathroom. Ryan's in his pajamas, crying and angry.

"*I liked her!*"

"I liked her, too."

"Then why?!"

"It just didn't work out, honey. Sometimes—"

"Why didn't it work out?"

"We were just a little too different, y'know?"

"Bullshit!"

"Ryan—"

"It's bullshit! It is!"

"I know. I'm sorry."

He breathes, sits on his bed, and looks down, sadly.

"I shouldn't've told you she was late."

I kneel down by the bed and look him in the eye.

"Listen to me," I say. "This has nothing to do with you."

"Well, I told you. And now she's gone."

"Ryan—don't even think that!"

But he curls up on his bed and looks at the wall.

"Dad . . . ?" he whispers. "You don't have to worry about me all the time."

"I worry about everything, Sport."

"You don't have to. And you don't have to find me a new mom."

I look at him, surprised. *Shit. Is that what I was doing?*

"I—I wasn't," I say. "Is that what you—do you want one?"

"No. I've already got one. Somewhere."

"I know."

"We're fine the way we are."

"That's absolutely right."

I hold him and rock him, slowly, until he falls asleep.

3:30 pm. A Sunday several weeks later. Stanhope A&P.

Ryan and I stopped going to the Price Chopper for obvious reasons. The A&P is more run-down, but they're renovating, and they've just put in a prepared food section. The place is decked out for the holidays and school kids are in the front of the store singing Christmas carols that play over the store loudspeakers.

Here at the A&P, the deli guys look like deli guys: big, hardy, white-haired men, butchers and ex-marines. They're all business. Not cute or chatty. They don't need to wear sweatshirts to make them look less provocative. And they certainly don't give out a lot of free samples of ham.

Ryan finds the bamboo carving boards.

"They're reinforced! Price Chopper had the normal ones, but these are reinforced!"

"Why do you want a bamboo chopping board so badly anyway?"

"Hot Wheels ramp!"

And so, the kids have finished and the grocery's turned on the canned music. It's a regular day again.

Angels we have heard on high

And I realize it's not canned music. It's a husky familiar voice.

Sweetly singing o'er the plains

And Ryan rushes to the front of the store, abandoning our cart and carving board. And there she is, dressed in sparkling white deli cutter's overalls, but with a red and white Santa's hat on and singing to a karaoke machine.

And the mountains in reply
Echoing their joyous strains

Ryan waves to her, maniacally. She grins and waves back, then finishes singing. The crowd claps and she comes over to us.

"Merry Christmas," she says.

"You sound great!" says Ryan.

"Thank you."

"Dad let me get the bamboo board!"

"Good. The ones here are better anyway—"

"They're reinforced!" they say in unison.

"Frankie!" calls one of the burly, all-business ex-marines.

"It was great seeing you guys again," she says. "Stop by and get some meat!"

She goes off, back to work. I realize, Ryan's right. I can't be scared all the time. No matter what happens.

Life's too short to be shy.

"Frankie!" I call out. "Do you—do you have any plans for dinner?"

She stares at me.

"Never mind," I say.

"No," she says. "I don't."

"Would you like to have dinner with us?"

"Only," she says, "if Ryan cooks"

Ryan looks at me, panicked.

"I don't cook that good," he says.

"It's okay," I say. "We'll help."

Manic Pixie Dream Girl Police

AT A STARBUCKS. FRANKLIN, LATE TWENTIES, SHEEPISH, lonely, depressed, nerdy, stands near MEG, a barista, early twenties, very cool, possibly with streaked colors in her hair. She makes him a latte.

FRANKLIN: So, uh . . . you like being a barista?

MEG: Sure! But I'm also into skydiving and surfing. I'm a veterinarian on the weekend—and I'm lead singer in an all-girl rock band! (*plays air guitar*) *Cranggg!* (*beat*) But you have to be careful cause a lot of people are totally fake! But I can spot phonies a mile away!

FRANKLIN: And, uh . . . what about me?

MEG: You are *totally* real.

FRANKLIN: Hey, this is gonna sound lame, but—
would you like to hang out sometime?

MEG: Like a date?

FRANKLIN: Uhm—

MEG: Absolutely!

FRANKLIN: Oh, wow. Great! That's—

*Suddenly, SIRENS BLARE, LIGHTS FLASH. Meg
freezes in place, and THREE WOMEN in camouflage riot
gear rush on. Franklin looks around, terrified.*

BECKY: Alright! Secure the area!

*Two of the women grab a now limp Meg and hold her.
BECKY, the chief, reads a summons to Franklin.*

BECKY: Franklin Delacourte?! (*beat*) This your
little play we're in?

FRANKLIN: Uh, yes . . . ?

BECKY: (*looking at summons*) Looks like you've
created a *Manic Pixie Dream Girl* to save
you from your pathetic little story?

FRANKLIN: (*confused*) Manic—?

BECKY: *Manic Pixie Dream Girl!* Wish fulfillment! Male fantasy! You've created some two-dimensional bippity boppity plaything to fall in love with you, unbelievable as that is, and rescue you from this sad gutter of an existence. (*to the others*) Alright! Take her away!

Franklin stops them.

FRANKLIN: Wait! Wait! Isn't a little escapism a good thing?! Don't I have some kind of artistic license?

BECKY: *Not today, buster!*

FRANKLIN: Wait! What—if I cut out the rock band—and the skydiving, and—give her a live-in mother who suffers from—dementia?

BECKY: (*impatient*) And?

FRANKLIN: And . . . make her considerably less interested in me?

Becky considers, waves away the other riot gear women, and rips up the summons.

BECKY: Alright. *But we're watching you!*

They leave. Meg comes back to life, but she seems much more normal, depressed and much less interested in Franklin.

FRANKLIN: So . . . about tonight?

BECKY: Oh, sorry I can't. I have to take care of my
demented mother.

Watering Plants

JEN WAS THE HOTTEST THING ON THE FLOOR.

And I was dancing with her and losing myself.

I had never in my life been to the kind of parties Keller Manyon held after—and sometimes *during*—work hours. They started early and went all night. It wasn't just the under-thirties. Everyone at the company partied hard. At the moment, the crowd was throbbing up and down to blaring, unrecognizable house music.

The party was at the gigantic loft apartment of K/M's Creative Director, Bob Caldwell. Looking at the place, it was hard to imagine a human being living there day to day. There was no apparent furniture or living space, just an open warehouse with random, ragged couches strewn about. Giant pop art pieces hung on the walls including an enormous black and white replica of Bob's most famous vodka ad—the one that probably bought this apartment for him and maybe even his mansion in Westchester, where his wife and teenage kids lived.

"*Greg!*" Bob yelled to me over the music. I'd come to know Bob a little beyond my regular duties at K/M in that I provided him with an endless supply of dime bags once or twice a week. Bob, with his shock of white hair and dark tan, held forth among a cluster of young employees.

"Have you seen Greg's band?!" he yelled to them. "He's lead guitar in the best band in the village!"

"Bass," I shouted, uselessly.

"*Motherfucker's awesome!*" he yelled.

"*You are the man!*" he yelled at me.

But Jen was the only reason I was there. We had flirted at the office a few times, or so I'd imagined. I could never really tell if she was just being playful. She was not the type I typically ended up with. On the dance floor, she writhed and shouted, but if you peeled away that drunken abandon—that sexy sloppiness—she was, at heart, a know-it-all, a prep, a Vassar girl.

At Keller Manyon, she was a junior art director.

And I was the guy that watered the plants.

I liked watering the plants, but I had a lot of jobs at the time. I played bass in Chrome Stitch, a blues funk band, which paid nothing, and I worked weekends and off-nights at Continental Thrift, a used clothing store, which paid slightly more than next to nothing. I did building services for 85 Fifth Avenue—which meant working almost exclusively for K/M every day, all week long. I did odd jobs, party and meeting set-ups, occasional catering. I reset lightly broken furniture and crooked artwork and did minor janitorial. And I helped during mail room emergencies.

But mostly I watered the plants.

Unlike all of my other occupations, watering the plants paid unbelievably well. It was a job you could do without moderating your appearance too much. As long as you looked modestly institutional, it didn't much matter if you had a thick, massive beard or tats everywhere—all of which I had.

💔

Jen and I had gone outside to get air and watch the snow beat down. She was frantically texting while cradling her beer bottle between her legs. I offered her a joint. She took a long drag and smiled at me.

"You have anything harder?" she asked.

"No," I said. "Sorry."

"No?" she said, surprised. "You?"

"Yeah, no," I repeated, politely.

"Shiiiiiiiit," she said, staring at me.

"Is that a problem?" I asked.

She shook her head.

"I dunno," she smiled. "I think I kinda like that."

I was spinning, trying to catch snow on my tongue and slipped and fell, which made her guffaw loudly. She helped me up, then pulled me close and kissed me. It was one of those kisses where the kiss separates you and whomever you're kissing from the rest of the world—just you and them alone on some hidden, cosmic island.

"Let's go to your place," she whispered to me, matter of factly.

"Okay," I said. "Uh, it's not—"

"What?"

"I mean, I wasn't expecting company. Like ever."

She grinned.

💔

She woke up around eight the next morning, bleary-eyed and disoriented.

"Oh . . . *oh shit*," she said.

Nearby, I was hunched over a beat-up, low-to-the-ground coffee table, separating seeds from a pound bag of

Northern Lights, which was approximately my Saturday morning routine. (And if Jen wasn't there, there'd have been cartoons on in the background.)

"Morning," I said.

"Hey," she said, burying her head back into the pillow.

I climbed next to her, cautiously.

"So . . . this happened," I pointed out.

"I see that," she said.

"Regrets?"

She peered at me through the pillow.

"Absolutely not," she said.

Slowly, she turned, sat up, and took in the full measure of my castle: frayed posters, dilapidated carpet, mangled band equipment, miscellaneous dope paraphernalia, and clothes strewn about everywhere.

"I tried to clean a bit before you got up," I said.

"Really?" she laughed.

"No," I said. "I didn't do anything."

"Jesus! What's that smell?" she gulped, suddenly.

"Space heater caught fire a couple weeks ago," I pointed to a blackened outlet across the room. Nearby was the stand-alone metal oil heater with a charred, melted rubber plug at the end of it. She gagged. "That's probably the residual smell. I wanted to fix it—"

"Just buy a new one!"

"Yeah, I should throw it out. I'm kind of used to the smell. It was worse a week ago, if you can believe it."

"God," she said, recoiling.

I got up and opened a window.

"Where's my phone?" she asked.

I handed it to her.

"It was buzzing all night, so I turned it off. That okay?"

"Sure."

"Who's Peaches?"

Peaches was the name that kept texting her all night.

"*My aunt Paula,*" she grumbled, annoyed.

"Want some breakfast?" I asked.

She grit her teeth, worried.

"I mean, go out for breakfast?"

"Absolutely," she said.

At a diner, two blocks away.

I had coffee and toast and watched as she devoured an oversized breakfast burrito and a large chocolate muffin. Her dark brown hair, knotted, she was an angelic, ragged mess.

"Stop staring," she said. "You're freaking me out."

"I feel like—" I started.

"Yeah?"

"I feel like—I dunno—I feel like I might not be see-ing you again."

She looked at me, surprised, pissed.

"*Why?*"

"It just seems like—this is a fluke or something."

"What?" she laughed. "I'm not good enough for you?!"

"For *me?*" I said. "*Wow.*"

She stared at me, pissed, confused. She hit me.

"Hey!" I said, grabbing her arm and holding it away. "Some of us don't work out ten times a week."

"I barely work out," she said, going back to her food. "I just burn all this off."

I sat back, watched her, looked out the window. Crowds passed by. Her phone buzzed.

"Jesus Christ!" she said, looking at the text.

"Your aunt?"

"All goddamn day long."

She turned the phone off, put it away. I looked at her.

"So . . . last night was real, then?" I asked.

"I don't know. Was it?"

"For me, yeah," I said. "I knew what I was doing."

She ate and drank, said nothing.

"So . . . you'd wanna go out again?" I said.

"Fuck yeah," she said.

We saw a lot of each other after that. She frequently came to gigs and brought friends from work or her African dance class. She hung out with me and the band. We made fun of people on the street and at work and we saw movies and drank and drank and smoked weed and drank, but not too much. Or maybe it was too much. Who knows? And we always ended up back at my place on my crap futon on the floor.

She had her own apartment, somewhere uptown in the seventies on the east side. But she never brought me there. Her father paid rent—*"half the rent!"* she'd correct me—but she seemed ashamed of its very existence. (So we both hated our apartments, but for very different reasons.) She didn't go there much herself unless she absolutely needed a change of clothes or to get work done.

Then there was Keller Manyon. We kept things on the down-low, but she was surrounded by talented, beautiful young copywriters and designers who made money hand over fist or who were on the verge of doing so. Folks who I liked, who treated me almost like an equal while I fixed their broken chairs, watered their plants, and sold pot to them.

Once, I was in Bob Caldwell's office, watering his geraniums. He was reviewing one of Jen's *Fila* mock-ups and offered me a lit jay.

"Thanks," I said. "Can't while I'm working."

"In three weeks," he brayed, "I'm gonna have that music spot for you, Greg. Swear to God, I'm gonna get you in production here. Hold me to it!"

"Thanks, Bob," I said, spraying the back edges of the leaves near the window.

His three-week music promise had been a broken record for well over six months. But I knew nothing about commercial music editing and couldn't hold a candle to his experienced production guys. So, I didn't give it much thought.

"*Jen!*" he barked.

And Jen was there, suddenly, holding a stack of illustrations wedged under her arm.

"You know Greg?" he asked.

She feigned confusion.

"The plant guy? Yeah," she said. "My plant's alive. So, good job, dude!"

"He's the *best* fucking plant guy!" said Bob. Then he pulled my cd out of his desk drawer and threw it at her.

"*Listen to it*. Fuckin' brilliant. He did the whole thing. Songs. Lead guitar."

"Just bass," I corrected.

"I'll give a listen," she said, po-faced. "I love new music. Especially bass."

I left them, closing the door and then heard laughing back inside. Was he offering her the joint? Was she taking it? And why not, if that's what the boss wants? Whatever it takes to keep ahead of the game. In some ways, I thought, she was just as messed up as he was.

In those first few intense weeks, she'd occasionally show up at my door drunk or crying, or drunk and crying and throw herself into my arms. Sometimes, I'd wake up to her staring at me or pulling on my hair, which she did all the time. More and more frequently she stayed at my place. Essentially, without any formal invitation, she moved in with me. Who was I to complain?

And I tried to clean the place up for her, but it was useless. There was just too much shit accumulated. She didn't seem to care. Still, it seemed like just a matter of time before she opened her eyes and decided to call it quits.

"Let's go to your place," I said abruptly one night.

We were sitting on the futon watching TV, eating Chinese, when I had my radical idea.

"What?"

"Let's go to your place."

"When?"

"Now."

"No. No no no no no no no . . ."

"Why not?"

"It's a dump."

"Bullshit."

"It's too sterile."

"For me?"

"No. Just . . . no."

"You don't want me up there?"

"It's not mine. This place is yours. It's a shithole—but it's *your* shithole. It's fully lived in."

"I feel like there's a part of you I don't even know. Your books—"

"I don't have books."

"How can you be an art director and not have books?"

"How can you be a fucking drug dealer and just sell pot?! What the fuck is that?"

I turned away from her.

"Shit. Shit, shit, shit. Greg," she said. "Come on. I'm sorry."

I turned back to her.

"When you leave here, you go somewhere I don't know anything about."

"I only go up to change for work or class if I *have* to. And usually not even then."

"I share my *only* space with you. But—"

"You're right," she said. "You're right. I don't share it with you."

"So?"

"I know. I just—I'm sorry."

I was speechless. I sat back against the wall, stared out the window.

"Don't you even fuckin' pout on me," she said. "C'mon, is this a deal-breaker?"

I said nothing. She kneeled up, got in my face.

"Is this a deal-breaker?"

"No," I said.

Two nights later, the band had a cancellation. I was restless and figured what the hell and took the subway up

to Seventy-Third and Third. The weather had dropped fifteen degrees and I was bundled in a heavy coat, scarf, and
boots. The area was a nondescript, dreary, dull part of
Manhattan, a place where some mildly well-off dad could
set his little girl up in an apartment without completely
bankrupting himself. She was right, I thought, it wasn't a
good neighborhood for her. She could do better.

I stopped and bought some lousy roses from a Korean
deli and pressed her buzzer. The intercom clicked on. She
was furious.

"*What the fuck,* Greg?" she snapped. "You promised."

"I know," I said, jovially. "Hey! I've got flowers."

I held the flowers up to the camera. She buzzed me in.

I took an elevator up to the fourth floor.

"You've got five minutes," she said. "I've got class and
I've got to get ready."

She glared as I dropped the coat, scarf, and flowers and
wandered through the place. It was small, Spartan, immaculate. A rollaway couch bed looked like it had never been
opened. There was a simple Ikea breakfast table with three
chairs, and a built-in kitchenette in the corner; off of the
kitchen was a small, plain bathroom. A second room was
empty except for half-opened boxes and a large walk-in
closet that contained the rest of her clothes. Everything
was shades of beige. Beige walls, lighter beige floors, *beigish*

cabinets. As she'd said, there were no books, no art supplies, nor even art on the walls. It was almost a hotel room except all the hotel rooms I'd stayed in had more character than this.

"So, that's it," she said, handing me my coat and moving me to the door.

I grabbed her and pulled her close, grinning.

"*Let's mess it up*," I said.

"I—have—class," she said.

"*Skip it*," I said.

I watched her pull back, retreat into herself, and realized it was useless. The moment was gone. I took my coat.

"You'll come down later?" I asked.

"Maybe," she answered, annoyed. "Maybe not."

Outside, I was torn. I was pissed, frustrated, confused. With no gig and nowhere to be, I had an urge to explore her neighborhood, to find out where she shopped, walked, and ate when she wasn't with me. I felt a chill, suddenly, and realized I didn't have my scarf. I headed back towards her place thinking I'd grab it before she left. As I approached, I saw a familiar figure standing outside her door, smoking a cigarette and pressing the buzzer, impatiently. Not thinking, I almost called out to him but then noticed the bottles of wine he held. I saw him text something on his cellphone and then, a moment later, the door came unlocked.

And Bob Caldwell went into Jen's building.

I didn't see her again for weeks. I parked myself in my apartment, didn't leave, didn't eat, didn't take calls, didn't let anyone in, drank heavily, smoked a tremendous amount of weed. I missed gigs to the point where the band threatened to kick me out if I didn't suck this shit up sometime soon.

After a week or so, I finally got up, got out, and walked around. I walked and walked and as the haze in my head began to clear, I realized how obvious it had all been. Really, they were in front of me the whole time. How could I have not seen it?

Of course, I stopped working at K/M altogether. I asked the agency who employed me for a building transfer, and they were good enough to move me over to a bland six-story office space in Murray Hill, where I worked mostly for an accounting firm. The employees there were forty or older. Everyone was quiet and exhausted and went home quickly after work. No all-night parties. Absolutely no one wanted a weekly pot delivery, but they certainly had lots of plants that needed watering.

I thought of leaving New York entirely. And why not? Nothing was keeping me here.

She was there the night of my first gig back. I knew she'd be there, because I'd heard she'd been coming by every night since the last time I'd seen her. I played anyway. I tuned her out and simply stared at the floor all night. On break, I went straight to the back, alone. I couldn't hide, though. And then she was there, suddenly, beer in hand.

"I'm sorry, Greg," she said. "I know I fucked up."

I shrugged, indifferent.

"It was all over before you even got there," she said. "I swear to God. I'd been trying to break it off with him for weeks. *You don't know how he hounded me*. I just—I just wanted to do well there. I didn't think it would go as far as it did. I know it's fucked up. I know."

"*Peaches?*" I said, looking at her, finally. "*Peaches?*"

"What could I say? If I had told you the truth you wouldn't have even talked to me."

"Of course I would've."

"No," she said. "You wouldn't."

She was right.

"I quit," she said. "I quit that night. I never went back. It's over."

I stared at her.

"I don't know what's bullshit with you and what's real," I said. "I have no idea who you actually are."

Tears welled up in her eyes. She tried to speak but saw my face flushed with rage and stopped. Taking a breath, she turned and walked—and then ran—out of the bar.

I went after her. (Maybe I shouldn't have. I probably shouldn't have. But I did.) I caught up to her a block or so down. She'd slipped and fallen on the ice. Two or three people were trying to help her. I knelt down to help her and slipped and then we were both on the ice, flailing to get a solid footing, but it was useless. We backed ourselves up against a rack of Christmas trees for sale on the filthy sidewalk and sat shivering on the cold ice.

"I shouldn't have gone up there," I said, sincerely. "It was a mistake."

"We should just get the fuck out of New York," she whispered to me.

"That—is a brilliant idea," I said.

She gripped my arm and held on, tightly, as forgiving flecks of snow fell softly and adorned us.

Circle in the Square

*A*T A CAFE. *TODD* AND *JENNIFER*, BOTH LATE TWENTIES, have coffee.

TODD: You're performing at *Circle in the Square*?

JENNIFER: Yeah.

TODD: You act?

JENNIFER: Mmm. I dance occasionally, too.

TODD: Wow . . . is this . . . so are you an extra . . . or—?

JENNIFER: I'm one of the leads.

TODD: You're one of the leads? One of the main—?

JENNIFER: Yeah.

TODD: So, you really act?

JENNIFER: I do.

TODD: Since when?

JENNIFER: I don't know, seventh grade?

TODD: You never told me you act.

JENNIFER: You never asked.

TODD: We've been connected at the hip for, like, six-seven weeks now. How could it not come up that you're performing at *Circle in the Square*?

JENNIFER: I don't know.

TODD: I mean, that's not something that people don't talk about. I know people that would kill to do anything at *Circle in the Square*!

JENNIFER: I know. I was one of them.

TODD: You just got the part?

JENNIFER: Yeah.

TODD: How long were you auditioning?

JENNIFER: Last three weeks.

TODD: Half the time I've known you?!

JENNIFER: Yeah.

TODD: I mean, hasn't your whole life been about this audition?

JENNIFER: Pretty much.

TODD: And you never told me?

JENNIFER: You didn't ask.

TODD: How would I know to ask? I don't go randomly asking people if they're auditioning at *Circle in the Square*.

JENNIFER: I don't like to talk about myself. I'm just—I'm a very private person.

TODD: But—I told you my whole life story!

JENNIFER: I know.

TODD: I completely opened up to you!

JENNIFER: I know.

TODD: You didn't tell me anything!

JENNIFER: It's fine.

TODD: It's not fine.

JENNIFER: I was happy to talk about you. You liked to talk about yourself and your life and the things you were doing, and that was fine. It was fun.

TODD: I shared things with you that I don't share with anyone—

JENNIFER: Well, I wouldn't go that far.

TODD: I trusted you.

JENNIFER: I know.

TODD: So, you didn't trust me?

JENNIFER: We were working together. It was a very productive experience. We did great work.

TODD: I just . . . I thought . . . I thought . . .

JENNIFER: What?

TODD: I don't know. I mean, you were giving me back massages . . .

JENNIFER: You were very stressed out.

TODD: I've been stressed out my whole life, but no one ever gave me back massages at work.

JENNIFER: Look, I think maybe you just got the wrong idea.

TODD: I guess so. I guess it was just work.

JENNIFER: It was work. It was very good work. We did great work. You should be very proud of yourself.

TODD: Yeah.

JENNIFER: Are we good here?

TODD: Sure.

JENNIFER: Good.

TODD: So, tell me about *Circle in the Square*.

JENNIFER: Oh, hey—I'm sorry. I can't. I have to go meet my boyfriend.

TODD: *You have a boyfriend?*

Hearts in Nature

M IKE—
So, I've decided. I'm going to Pokhara.

I don't know how to say this more delicately—not that delicate has ever been my strong suit—but I wanted to be honest with you. I've made up my mind. Pokhara is happening.

So.

So, first of all, *I love you.* You know that. I know that doesn't help or make anything better or easier, but I do. I love you—completely, totally, and with all my heart. I don't want you to wait for me. I want you to do what you need to do. Put me out of your mind. Live your life.

I'm not doing this to hurt you or run away from you. As you've heard me say a zillion times—*I have to do this.* I realize now I will never have the courage or freedom to do this again. If I don't do it, I'll come to resent and hate myself, and would likely come to resent and hate you, too. I won't let that happen, Mike.

I wanted to put this down on actual paper, to try to explain how I came to this. What finally pushed me over the cliff these last two weeks was that terrible book on my coffee table, the one my grandmother wrote: *Hearts in Nature*. Yes, it's an awful, schmaltzy thing. It's just that . . . I don't know. When I look at it now, I look at it differently. Something in me has changed.

Gramma gave me that first edition of the book when I was ten. I don't know whether or not she anticipated the unbelievable success it would become or that it would spawn a hateful industry of cards and mugs and more coffee table books and calendars. Oh my God—all those stupid, goddamn *Hearts in Nature* calendars everywhere. *Everywhere!* Tacky and gauche. Naomi actually found an old cat calendar the other day from the early twenties, the ones they say everyone used to have before all of Gramma's *Hearts in Nature* shit took off. Before this there were, at the very least, ubiquitous kittens.

Anyway, about a year before she died, back while I was still in high school, she told me that these cheesy desk-calendar things were not what she had originally intended. When she first started collecting pictures for the book, she was honestly looking for . . . something. For meaning, beauty, spirituality; for actual *hearts in nature*.

She grew up extremely poor, you know? She didn't have money to travel or leave the US. However, that didn't stop her from doing everything she could to help people all the time; whether it was volunteering her PT services at nursing homes or teaching meditation classes. She was always giving something away. Everything, really. It made grandpa crazy, but no one could stop her.

Did you know that she always wanted to go to Nepal? When the books first came out, she only set aside X percent for me and my family. Like less than five percent. The rest she gave to charity—even the future profits. The cheese factor only kicked in when she realized that mass producing the things would allow her to give exponentially to charity.

However, I realized over the last two weeks that if she'd left for Nepal when she was my age, she'd never have made the books. Because she would have found herself out there.

Why did she stay? To take care of my father? Was she too poor to go? Or did fear or complacency keep her stateside? Who knows?

I looked through the book again with all the pictures of rocks that look like hearts; and leaves and clouds and streams and everything that just look like hearts. We used to make fun of those pictures because those hearts—the cute, valentine-y kind she was depicting—don't actually *exist* in nature. And you know she had admitted that to me, that even in that first book she manipulated about twenty percent of the pictures. Moving rocks and leaves to make them more heart-y. It wasn't till she sold the rights that the new owners just started manipulating everything digitally.

But in that first book, Mike, there *is* something there: a yearning. Love. Spirituality. Hope. I couldn't see it when I was ten or thirteen. I just saw stupid hearts, but I see it now. I think it was her way of finding herself out there. And I think hers was the biggest heart in nature of all.

This has been upsetting for my dad, too. Ever since I told him he's just been heartsick. I saw him sing last night, and there was so much pain in his voice. Listening to him, I couldn't stop crying. In fact, he had the whole crowd in tears. He's terrified of me going, you know. He's convinced he's never going to see me again. But deep down, I think he knows this is the right thing for me to do.

So, I'm packed. Not bringing much. I have my ticket, my passport. I've already gotten some early assignments about what I'm supposed to be doing: rebuilding housing in a village, teaching kids English.

So, I'm leaving Thursday.

Maybe I'll make a difference. Maybe I won't. Maybe it'll be a complete waste of time, but I have to try.

I hope to be gone only a year. I honestly don't know what will happen after that, but I'd like to see you when I come back. I don't expect anything. Maybe just a smile and a cup of coffee. That would be plenty.

I'd like to write to you, if you're okay with that. After I get settled and start finding my way around, I'll post pictures, if they let me. I'll send you the links.

And yes, I promise—no hearts in nature.

Except for mine.

I love you.

Claire.

The Christmas Catalog

HOLIDAYS AT MY MOTHER'S BOOKSHOP WERE ALWAYS festive. A stunning tree stood near the front entrance with dozens of elegant, empty, gift-wrapped boxes at its base. Non-denominational lights—Christmas reds and greens along with Chanukah blues and whites—lit up her windows. Holiday tunes crackled across her broken-down cassette-driven sound system. Our family flocked there. Mom ran the place. Molly came in after school to run the cash register. Gramma waddled in in the evening, all made up in her red cape, ready to give customers various suggestions on books she'd never read. Dad came on Sundays to talk to the folks buying the *New York Times*. I came in to mop.

Molly and I fought to see who would get to spray fake snow on the windows, the door, the counters, and on books.

Unfortunately, the shop never did much business. It was bought with "seed money" Mom inherited from my grandfather. After six months, if the store couldn't start paying for itself, my father would have to subsidize the rent and overhead and any employee costs. In three years, the shop had never made a dime.

It was located on a quiet, non-descript side-street at the edge of town, less than a block from the railroad station. Sandwiched between Joe's Meat Market—a shoebox of a deli with inch-thick dust on everything, including Joe—and an abandoned tchotchke store, it was dismal but quaint. To find yourself at this bookshop, you had to be either incredibly lost or a close, personal friend of my mother's. All of her customers were both.

Besides the location, sales were perpetually awful because of the poor selection—and sheer lack—of books. If you were looking, for example, for the complete works (or *any* works for that matter) of Dickens, Hemingway or Mailer, you weren't likely to find them here. Nor were you likely to find histories of Rome, self-help books, reference books, Isaac Asimov, or much Dr. Seuss. Of current novels and non-fiction Mom would get only a few copies as she just wasn't inclined to maintain "popular" books and didn't feel it necessary to pander to some "mass" audience. If you really needed that stuff, she could special order it. (*Anything in print in six to eight weeks!*) No, she had no interest in being just another big bookstore.

Mom's forte was Art Books. Big, out-of-print, sixty-dollar, coffee table Art Books. Beautifully bound, exquisitely printed, covering classic and contemporary; local shows and exhibits from around the world. Lavish, gorgeous books that no one wanted, and no one could afford. She loved them. Yes, her cooking, poetry and crossword book sections weren't bad. And her bookmark and bookplate sections ran two aisles wide and were possibly the best in the country. But all were window dressing for her Art Books.

💔

And so, the shop lost money and more money and more money. Then Dad would re-invest and take a write-off. He'd urge Mom to push the more reader-friendly books, but nothing changed. In the last few months before Christmas, there was always a bit of unspoken tension in the house. Dad would come home from work moody and quiet, occasionally grumbling about how, at work, he still hadn't gotten what he deserved. Mom told us that he had wanted to start his own business but didn't have the finances, but he never mentioned the ongoing cost of the bookshop; never suggested it might be time to pack it in.

This particular Christmas, however, things were going to be different, because this year Mom had decided to send out a *Christmas Catalog*.

This became *The Big Project*. It was to be a huge holiday catalog, just like Shillito's, but solely for us and our shop. With green mistletoe-trimmed borders and yule-log browns, it would be expensive and *plush*, but worth it. It would grab people—both locally and throughout the greater city—and invite them to come celebrate the holidays with us and our books. The catalog promised a lavish, well-stocked selection of popular titles. It contained a gift section, a children's section. Mystery *and* science fiction, a lengthy center section gave details on location, hours, and free gift wrapping. In the back were brief, informative pages: a condensed History of The Shop (it'd been open three years, with two different owners); a Questions and Comments page; and a Calendar of Events for the winter season, including eggnog parties, a children's reading series (for which she'd bought a new reading chair), and the big event: a real, live Author's Book Signing with a well-known elderly feminist poet.

Mom spent months meeting with printers and assembling advance notices and pictures. Holiday t-shirts and tote bags were ordered, and a giant, new, gift-wrapping machine was purchased. Not since Summer inventory had things been this exciting!

Then the catalogs arrived. Thousands. Crisp, glistening, multi-colored and with no discernable typos. We set them out in huge stacks across the dining room table, arranged by zip code. Then, standing in classic Ford assembly-line formation, we affixed sheet after sheet of mailing labels. That Saturday, Dad and I hauled them to the post office and sent them on their way, to friends, family, strangers, housewives, professional businessmen, local politicians, and celebrities. Mom bought radio time, announcing the holiday catalog— *free!*—just come to the shop and get one, or call us and give us your address and we'll mail you a copy free of charge. It was easily the greatest affair the little shop ever had.

This catalog was going to change things. It would put the shop on the map. Mom knew it, and then she could really build on her dream: tear up the rotted, peeling floor; replace the windows; put up a new sign; acquire the tchotchke store next door and knock down the walls.

Expand! Do things right! Maybe set up a little cafe with outdoor tables. A modern sound-system—or, at least, pick up some new cassettes. Proper display cases—huge, finished, oak monsters—to give the Art Books the presentation they truly deserved. Then, build up a real, year-long clientele. The catalog would be the beginning of all of this.

At first, they came in dribs and drabs, merely out of curiosity, as if searching for the odd, potato-sculpture museum, eight exits off the highway. They came and looked and whispered, tracked in snow and slush and knocked racks of bookplates over. They left crossword books in the poetry section and poetry books in the restroom. They took catalogs and drank egg-nog and left, buying nothing. Mom became restless.

"Don't mop while customers are here!" she said to me. "They'll slip and break their neck!"

Cool, I thought.

Finally, magically, on the Saturday afternoon just before Christmas, people actually started to buy things.

"A book on Cezanne? I just saw the show in Montreal!" said a woman in white fur.

"Wonderful catalog! Wonderful!" said another.

"Times Crossword!" said a 340-lb. man, gurgling smoke from a pipe. He angled near Gramma. "1963 Series. Spiral bound. Yellow. Need it today!"

"Of course you do!" she replied, smiling and escorting him to the back.

A gaggle of rosy-faced teens, hired carolers, hovered outside, lurching loudly through *O Tannenbaum.*

More customers came in. The woman in white fur bought the Cezanne book and six bookmarks. The pipe-smoker bought three crossword books and special ordered three more. Two little girls fought to sit in the new chair in the children's section. Three people actually tried to pay for catalogs. One woman tried to buy all of the shop's Christmas cassettes. Things were hopping. They bought bookplates, holiday cards, cookbooks, and tote bags. They drank eggnog and stood outside, watching the carolers.

The elderly feminist poet came in, tearful.

"This catalog is *so* beautiful! *And my picture!* No one's ever honored me like this. It's the best gift I could have asked for!"

My mother cried and they hugged each other. Molly and I argued over who's turn it was to mop.

The sun sank and the crowd thinned. The glow of a most successful day filled Mom. Just as she began peeking into the cashbox to see how well we'd really done, she noticed, in the doorway, a small, grinning man in tweed jacket and horn-rimmed glasses, looking wide-eyed into the shop as if seeing books for the first time. He had a look of utter, devilish excitement and breathed the entire place in, giddily. This was a man who was going to buy books. *A lot of them.* He flipped through the bookmarks, eagerly, laughing and making mental notes.

"Can I help you?" asked Mom.

"Oh no, no! I'm fine!" He said, disappearing into the cookbooks aisle.

Gramma moved to help him, but Mom grabbed her and redirected her towards an old teacher lost in Pet Rearing. Out of the corner of her eye, she followed the tweed man as he darted section to section, giggling and

staring at titles, *but never taking a single book off the shelf.*
What was he looking for?

Then all of a sudden, she heard a loud gasp! *The Art Books!* He'd found them. From the counter, Mom saw Art Book after Art Book disappear, slipping down into greedy, unseen hands.

"He's taking the whole section," she whispered to me, anxiously. "He's taking my Art Books! We won't have any left!"

She moved to help him, but teen carolers, worn and ruddy, blocked her way. She pulled out an envelope and handed it to them.

"Thank you so much," she said, abruptly. "We'll see you tomorrow?"

They nodded and left. Then, there before her was the little tweed man, empty-handed and eyes afire.

"You *must* be the owner," he gulped, excitedly.

"Yes," she answered.

"Of course, you are! You have quite a shop here! Quite a shop! And the catalog! It must've taken *weeks* to put together!"

"Oh . . . well . . ."

"*Splendid work!* Splendid! This shop has quite a unique point-of-view! You realize that? Quite the personal stamp!"

"Well, I—"

"Of course, you do! Of course, you do! Few stores have a true point-of-view! Most are just the faceless facades of the bled, barren spirits behind them. But this shop *has character! Personality!* This powerful little shop all alone in this desolate . . ." He recoiled, emotionally. "Simply marvelous."

"Thank you," said Mom, feeling flush. No one had ever spoken to her like this. She'd always thought of herself and her shop as poor, artsy outsiders. She watched as he paged through the catalog.

"Special orders! Out of print tomes! And you got *her!* Wonderful poet! Bravo!"

Mom leaned forward. She couldn't take it, anymore.

"But . . . wouldn't you like to—to *buy* something?!"

He looked at her, eyes twinkling.

"Oh yes," he said.

A little while later, Dad entered, wrapped in a thick, wool sweater with boxes and bags under each arm. He stared at the crowd: Molly and Gramma bringing wrapped books to customers; women rushing in and out; one boy, teetering at the eggnog, refilling his sixth cup; and Mom, amid them, thrilled. She came over and embraced Dad. He smiled.

"I've got something for you," he said.

In the back of the shop he withdrew an envelope and handed it to her. She opened it up and covered her mouth. It was the deed to the abandoned tchotchke store next door.

"I've just made a down payment," he said. "Now, you can tear down the walls! Expand! Send catalogs all year long!"

She turned away. Tears ran down her face. From the desk, she pulled out another envelope and handed it to him. He withdrew the papers and stared at them, stunned.

"You . . . you sold the shop?"

She nodded, slowly.

"A man came in—and—and made me an offer. The store, books, everything. He had that same look I had, when we first bought it—that fire in his eyes, that vision. And he offered much more than it's worth. I think."

"But . . . you love this shop."

She smiled.

"And now, someone else can try their luck." She looked into his eyes. "Now we can invest in you."

The last customer left. Mom locked the doors. It was dark and the Christmas tree and window lights—reds and greens and the Chanukah blues and whites shone brightly.

Dad took the mop from me and went at it, himself. Gramma and Molly came out and we all stared at the tree and the window.

Outside, snow fell, and a train crossed the tracks, filling the air with its *clackety-clackety-clack*.

The Forrest Gump
Question

*H*AL *AND MARNIE, ON A BLIND DATE, MEET FOR THE first time over drinks at a restaurant.*

MARNIE: Hal?

HAL: Yes! You must be Marnie?

They sit, both enthusiastic.

MARNIE: *So* nice to meet you! To be honest, I
was a little nervous.

HAL: Oh sure. Me, too.

MARNIE: This is your first time using the *Love
Always* app?

HAL: Yeah. Using any app, actually. Yours?

MARNIE: Same! It's a little weird.

HAL: Yes, it is.

MARNIE: This place is lovely.

HAL: Thanks. Thank you.

Long awkward pause.

MARNIE: Do you mind if I ask you a question?

HAL: Shoot.

MARNIE: Did you see *Forrest Gump*?

HAL: Oh. Uh—the movie?

MARNIE: Yes. I just saw it again last night for, like, the fifteenth time—

HAL: Uh huh.

MARNIE: Wasn't it just the best movie? It's so moving! Didn't you love it?

HAL: Well—y'know—I can barely remember it. I saw it when it first came out.

MARNIE: You just—you just saw it the once?

HAL: Yeah. Anyway. (*beat*) So, why don't we order?
    The brussel sprouts are so—

MARNIE: Sure. Sure. In a minute. *But didn't you
    love it?* It was so . . . oh, I don't
    know . . . *special!*

HAL: Uhm. You know, I'm really not much of a critic.

MARNIE: But you *loved Forrest Gump*?

HAL: I'm—I'm not even sure how to answer that.

MARNIE: Well, I'll tell you what—I'll just assume
    you did.

HAL: Okay.

MARNIE: Loved it! Loved it, loved it, loved it!
    Like I did.

Hal looks around, uncomfortably.

HAL: You know, I used to come here for the cala-
    mari. Remember it was pretty good, too!

She reaches out and takes his arm, imploringly.

MARNIE: But you know, I think I'd like to hear it from you. *You know?* It would mean so much more to me.

HAL: Say—you know what was good? *Jaws.* That was good! Remember that? Big shark? Scary!

MARNIE: Tell me you liked it.

HAL: Richard Dreyfus in an unforgettable role! And Robert Shaw as Quint! *We're gonna need a bigger boat!*

MARNIE: Please tell me you liked it. Please. Please. *Gump!*

HAL: I always heard it was just a big puppet, you know? The shark?

MARNIE: Please tell me. Please tell me.

HAL: Not a—a real puppet, y'know. A—a—a mechanical puppet. I mean, not like a robot—don't think they had those back then—

MARNIE: *Tell me!*

She gets up, anxiously—stands over him.

HAL: So, climate change seems like a real thing,
      huh?

She grabs the back of his shoulders and shakes him.

MARNIE: *TELL ME!*

(Beat)

He turns and looks at her matter-of-factly.

HAL: I hated it.

*She lets go of him, and takes a step back, stunned. She plops
back into her seat, confused, heartbroken. He stares at her.*

HAL: Geeze . . . this always happens.

MARNIE: You didn't like *Forrest Gump*?

HAL: Is that what I said?

MARNIE: I'm not sure.

HAL: No. No. I *didn't* like *Forrest Gump*. I didn't.
      And honestly, I don't think it deserved the
      Oscar. *(calling out)* Check, please!

MARNIE: (*despondent*) I don't know what to say.

Hal gets up, offers her his hand.

HAL: It was nice meeting you. I wish this didn't change things. But—too late for that.

She looks away from his hand. He looks around for the waiter.

MARNIE: I'm sorry. I'm sorry. I'm still processing—

She starts crying quietly to herself. No waiter comes. Hal sits back down, but not quite completely down.

HAL: Look, there are probably a lot of guys out there who liked it. I'm sure you'll find one of them.

He does the "check, please" hand gesture in the air to someone offstage.

MARNIE: (*mumbling*) Ididn'teither.

HAL: Excuse me?

MARNIE: I said—I said—I—I didn't like it, either.

HAL: (*skeptical*) Really?

She nods.

HAL: You're sure? You're not just saying that?

MARNIE: No. No! Well, parts of it. The ping-pong. But no—no— (*shivers, confessing*) *I really didn't like it.*

HAL: Uh huh?

MARNIE: There's always just been so much pressure to like it!

HAL: (*compassionate*) I hear you.

MARNIE: It's always been so confusing.

HAL: It's true.

She takes his hand.

MARNIE: Thank you, for being honest.

HAL: Of course.

MARNIE: Y'know, I sense that while *I* didn't like it, you really didn't like it.

He nods.

MARNIE: And I appreciate your candor!

HAL: Sure.

MARNIE: (*pulling back*) Look at me! Look at me! I'm so stupid. I'm so sorry.

HAL: It's fine. It's absolutely—

MARNIE: Could we just forget all this? Could we start over?

HAL: Sure.

MARNIE: Hal. Hal?

HAL: Hal.

MARNIE: Hal. You know, you're *so* honest. I find that quite attractive.

HAL: (*surprised*) Really?

MARNIE: Yes. Yes, I do. (*beat*) May I ask you a personal question?

HAL: Of course.

MARNIE: Did you see *Pretty Woman*?

HAL: (*calling out*) Check, please!

Come Home Soon

OFTEN, I WAKE IN THE MIDDLE OF THE NIGHT WITH TRE-MENDOUS ANXIETY. I FEEL LIKE THE FAMILY IS MUCH larger—there are more kids, and something is wrong. But who's in charge? Where is the leader of the family? The parent? The father? Meaning *my* father—not me. But then I remember in a flash—I'm the senior person here—the Daddy. But I panic even more. Why? What's wrong? Is everyone okay? And then I remember—it's just us. Just me and Jake and Kit. (And my mom half the time.) And that's it. Everyone's fine. The anxiety passes. For a couple days, anyway.

The house is a mess. I try to keep it straight, but I'm fighting against my base instincts. I know I have to do laundry, give Kit baths. I know I could let my mom do it, but it's not right. No, I just have to regimen myself. Do it. Must be what it's like to be divorced—except I can't date on the side. Not that I'd have the energy to.

Jake sits in his room, playing guitar, brooding. Do Not Disturb, Please.

"Did you write something for her again?"

"I'm sending her a disc." He holds up a cd. "It's just some stuff I did. It's not so good. She'll probably like it."

💔

Kit screams out in the middle of the night, hysterical.

"Daddy! Daddy!"

I get in bed with him. Guess I'm not the only one with anxiety.

"It's okay. Shh. Shh."

"Is Mommy home?"

"No, honey. Not yet."

"When's Mommy coming home?"

"In a few weeks. Maybe January."

"She'll be home at Christmas?"

"No."

"Why not?"

"It's not her turn. They have to take turns and it's someone else's turn. They need her."

He trembles and starts crying again.

"Shhh . . ."

I spend the rest of the night in his little bed, cramped against the wall. In the morning I plunk down Advil. I've been plunking down Advil day after day for the past six weeks. I'm sure I'm developing an ulcer.

Just a few more hours and we're off to sunny, sunny Florida. We're all packed. Just pick up the kids, get 'em on a plane. Then my folks can take over for a while. And I can sleep for days.

The next day at work. My phone vibrates in my pocket.

"Mom? I'm in a meeting. Can I call you—"

"What's wrong?" asks Bruce, my boss, overhearing the conversation.

"My day care called her. Kit's running a fever. Shit. Shit. She just got off the plane in Florida."

I talk into the phone. "No—don't come back. That's crazy. We'll be fine, Mom! Don't be stupid! We're fine! Look—I'll get him! I'll call you later."

I hang up. Bruce looks at me hang dog, pityingly.

"I know your mom's been staying with you."

"We were all going down to their place in Boca Raton. She flew down this morning. The kids and I are flying down tonight. I gotta go, Bruce. I'm sorry."

"Go! Go. Do whatever you have to, Mike."

"I'm sorry."

"No big deal!"

"I should just quit, Bruce. I just—it's too crazy—I'm not getting anything done. I'm not being effective."

"Mike. You're doing fine. It's the holidays. Don't worry about it. Do what you need to do."

In the car I checked in with day care. They're giving him Advil. We're all taking Advil. I call Nelson.

"What's the update?"

"Mike! Hey. Good to hear from you!"

"What've you got?"

"Well, here's the thing. There's a group—a coalition of families—they started with a petition but they're talking about a lawsuit against the military. Looks like we could get—I dunno—six—seven families involved."

"Just six or seven? That's it?!"

"That's pretty good, Mike. Not everyone wants to make this as public as you do."

"What if we go to the press?"

"Well, I wouldn't do that."

"Why not?"

"Well, it can work for you or it can work against you. And if it works against you—it can kill you."

"What does that mean?"

"The last thing you want is for them to paint a picture of Maggie as someone who's trying to get out of the system."

"She shouldn't be *in* the system!"

"I know that, but—"

"She finished her tour three months ago, Nelson! She did 18 months! She finished! Her obligation's over! She doesn't owe them anything! She's not some fucking deserter!"

"I know that, Mike. I'm not talking about you or me, here. But some people could take it as—as *favoritism*—on the government's part. Why single *her* out? Move *her* to the head of the line?"

"She's got two kids! She's got a fucking four-year-old!"

"I know, Mike. But some of the other mothers over there don't even have a Mike Olsen waiting back at home. Some of the kids are being raised by grandparents, neighbors, *foster parents*—if you're lucky, maybe somebody'll be sympathetic. But it might not go that way. I've looked into this, Mike. I'm just being honest with you."

"Look—just do whatever you need to do. Okay? Do whatever it takes."

"You bet. Let me make some calls. Call some of these other families. See what's up."

"Great. Great. You do that."

"Mike, listen. Y'know—there *are* other people out there—women—even a few men—who are in the same position as you. Support groups? Might help to find out who they are and—"

"Yeah. Thanks. I'm already in three support groups. Not to mention taking my kids to soccer and guitar tutoring and trying to keep my fucking job at the same time. But thanks for the suggestion. Just get my wife back for me, please?"

"I'll make those calls. Have a happy holiday, Mike."

"You too."

I pick up Kit in the school office. He's beet red, miserable, being rocked back and forth by Miss Kelly, a cute twenty-something in a day care sweatshirt with red and green Christmas pins hanging off her chest like ornaments. Tears streak down Kit's face. He reaches out to me. He's burning up.

"Is Mommy home?"

"No, honey. Shh. Everything's fine. We're going home."

"I gave him the Advil," says Kelly. "Call me if you need anything."

Kit falls asleep in the car. At home, I put him to bed. I spend the next hour yelling at airline customer service reps who don't want to refund three plane tickets. I catch my reflection in the hall mirror. I'm as red as Kit. I desperately want to lose my shit and explode at someone—and no one's more deserving than inconsiderate airline customer service drones who are charging me more than $300 to reschedule a grand's worth of unused children's airline tickets. It might even be healthy to vent at this person, but I have to remind myself that I can't do that. I can't lose my cool. I have to get through this. Remain centered. It's just money. It's not important. This sucks, but I've been through worse than this. It's not a crisis. Not yet, anyway. And I still have to deal the presents I already sent on to Florida . . . and Jake.

Jake comes in excited, bouncing off the wall.
"What's going on?! Where's Kit?"

"Jake. C'mere."

He looks at me. I don't have to say a word. He knows and he's angry—angry at me, at Maggie, at school, the world, the government. He's too smart. That's his problem. He's not blissfully ignorant like every other twelve-year-old in his class. When I was twelve my friends were stealing candy and cigarettes and hood ornaments. And they were just bored! You wouldn't even have described them as dysfunctional back then. Jake is smart and creative and incredibly, incredibly angry. How dangerous a combination is that?

"Kit's got a fever," I say.

"God-dammit!"

"Jake—"

"It's not fair!"

"I know."

"How bad is he? Can he travel?"

"He's got a 102-degree fever."

"So, what does that mean?"

"It means we're staying home."

"Can I go by myself?"

"No."

"Why not?"

"You're twelve."

"Gramma can meet me at the gate. It's no big deal!"

"Jake—no. I want us all together over the holidays."

"We're not all together! We're never all together! Why should we start now?!"

He runs to his room, slams the door. He's right. Why should he suffer with me? Maybe I should let him go alone. He could take care of himself. He's twelve—but he might as well be sixteen. Shit—I was alone on a plane when I was twelve, but that was the '70's. That was before you had to take off your shoes to get on an airplane.

No. No. Forget it. Not at an airport over the holidays. Where I'd have to let him out of my sight. I can't explain to Maggie that I let him get on a plane by himself, and I don't want us separated. He's just going to have to understand. I'll have to make it up to him.

I go in his room to try again. He's on his cell phone.

"Jake—I want to make this work for us, okay?"

He looks up at me with a mix of hate, resilience, and pity. No one looks at me without pity, anymore. Not even my son.

"Danny says I can go with him and his family to Mt. Koda for the weekend. His dad says if it's okay with you, they've got the extra room."

Shit. What can I say? At least it's supervised.

"You're all packed up for the beach!"

"I got out all my sweaters. I've got Danny's dad on the phone!"

He hands me the phone.

"Phil? You don't have to—I know. You've *really* got the room?"

Jake looks at me, hopefully.

"You're sure it's not going to be too much for you? The two of them together? Uh huh?"

I nod at Jake, approvingly. He glows. At least that's something.

"I owe you, Phil. Thanks. Let me know what the cost is. I'll get you back. Merry Christmas."

I hang up.

"Thanks, Dad!"

"They're coming in an hour," I say. "You're going to miss your mom's call."

He keeps packing. Tears start running down his face.

"I know. Tell her I miss her. A lot."

I hug him and he grabs me tightly.

"I know it's not your fault, Dad. I know it, but I gotta get outta here. I feel like I'm going crazy. I gotta do something. Get outta here—get my mind off it. Something. Something. I'm sorry. I'm sorry."

"I know, Jake. I know. You're right. You're completely right. It's the best thing. I wish I could go with you. It'll be good for you."

"Thanks, Dad. I love you."

"I love you, too, Jake."

"Maybe if Kit gets better you guys could come meet us?"

"Yeah. Maybe."

An hour later and he's gone.

Kit wakes up, crying, but falls back asleep, thankfully. I'm exhausted. At 6:30, Maggie calls.

"Thought I'd call before you jumped on the plane!"

"No jumping tonight," I say. I tell her everything.

"I delivered a baby today," she says.

"Iraqi?"

"Half and half. One of our boys knocked up a townie."

"He do the right thing?"

"They got married in the clinic this morning. Birth is the only good thing that happens here."

"I feel sorry for the baby."

"Yeah. I feel sorry for all the kids here. And the soldiers. And the locals."

"And us," I remind her.

"There's people that have it worse than us, Mike."

Why does everyone feel the need to tell me that all the time?

"You wouldn't believe the way these people live. It's awful."

"You hear anything on your end?"

"They say they've requisitioned personnel, but—"

"They always say that."

"We got two new doctors this week."

"Anyone go home?"

"No. Not from here. It can't be much longer, Mike. It can't be."

"I miss you, honey. The kids miss you terribly."

"I know. I miss you, too. Mike, you're sure you're okay with Kit?"

"Yeah."

"I can't believe I missed both of them. Shit. Some fuckin' Christmas."

"Yeah."

"I'll call Sunday."

"Call Sunday night. Jake'll be home by then."

"You did the right thing, Mike. He needed it."

"Yeah."

"I love you.

"I love you, too, honey."

"Merry Christmas."

Kit sleeps across my lap as I watch *A Christmas Story*. That's the one about the little kid who just wants a B-B gun for Christmas. I first saw that when Mags was pregnant with Jake and we were still living in our little apartment in Portland. Mag was in her third trimester and having a lot of pain. She fell asleep across my lap and I watched the movie with the sound off, a warm, uneventful moment. The kid in the movie opens up all his presents. No B-B gun. Then the father says look in the back, over by the corner. And there it is, all wrapped up in a long box, hidden the whole time.

Three weeks ago, we were all watching TV—my mom, Jake, and me. Kit was asleep. And a story comes on the news. Insurgents near Abu Ghraib have taken hostage an American doctor from the 118th Medical Battalion clinic. Maggie's clinic, and the hostage is a woman. The media, the American government won't release the name of the hostage. I spend all night on the phone talking to the military. What information do you have? What are they doing? Why can't you identify her? Just tell me if it's Maggie. Tell me if it's Jake and Kit's mother. All night long.

Nothing. Nothing. Until it's all over. No. No—don't worry. Rest easy. They've identified the body. It's okay. It's not her.

Not this time.

Four in the morning. I'm freezing, still lying on the couch. Kit's still lying across me but the blanket's slipped onto the floor. Kit doesn't notice, but my teeth are chattering. I hear a door open. Someone's downstairs.

My heart beats like a trip hammer. Someone's in the house at four in the morning? The day before Christmas? A burglar? A neighbor? Jake? Maggie? The door to the TV room creaks open. I hold my breath, pretend to be asleep.

It's my mom.

"Mom?" I whisper, not realizing how out of it I am.

"I caught the red eye back," she says.

"You didn't have to come back. You're ruining your holiday."

"It's not a holiday without you and the boys, Mike. C'mon. You two need to get to bed."

She picks up Kit, who curls up in her arms.

"I packed up the gifts and brought 'em back, too."

"Thanks, Mom," I say. "You're the best."

I watch her gently put Kit to bed. He's already improving, cooling down, breathing evenly. Who needs Florida?

I get into bed. Alone.

Things will work out. They always have. They always do.

She'll be home soon.

I just have to believe that.

The Dolphin

DERRICK AND JOHN COME OUT OF A THEATRE ONTO the street, in mid-conversation. John stops suddenly to stare, amazed, at a giant, offstage ceramic dolphin.

> DERRICK: And I didn't find the characterization
> at all believable. Especially in the
> second act, when it was obvious—

JOHN: Hey! Hey! Look at that dolphin!

Derrick stares at John, extremely annoyed, and walks away from him, down the street.

DERRICK: Never mind.

John chases after him.

JOHN: What? What were you saying?

DERRICK: Forget it—I don't feel like repeating myself—

JOHN: Derrick—Derrick—I'm sorry. (*beat*) I said I was sorry.

DERRICK: You don't even know what you did.

JOHN: I know what I did.

DERRICK: What did you do?

JOHN: I stopped to look at the dolphin.

DERRICK: You have no idea.

JOHN: Could we just stop? Could you just drop it?

DERRICK: Could I stop?! Could I drop it?!

JOHN: Yes. Could you drop it?

DERRICK: It's not about you? It's about me?!

JOHN: It's about both of us, obviously, or we wouldn't be arguing.

DERRICK: You're right and I'm always wrong.

JOHN: You said that. I didn't say that. You said that.

DERRICK: You said, "Could I drop it?"

JOHN: That's not what I meant.

DERRICK: Of course not. You never mean what
you say.

JOHN: Sometimes I do. Most times I do. This
wasn't one of those times.

DERRICK: How am I supposed to know when
you mean something and when you
don't?

JOHN: You can ask me. And then we can argue
about it for a few hours. That always clears
things up.

DERRICK: So, now, I'm making us argue?

JOHN: Yes!

Derrick walks further ahead. John chases after him.

JOHN: I just wanted to look at the dolphin!

Derrick turns.

DERRICK: I don't care about the fucking dolphin!

Derrick turns back and continues walking.

JOHN: Whatever I did! I'm sorry!

DERRICK: You're just trying to get out of it!

JOHN: Right!

DERRICK: So, don't apologize! It's meaningless!
It's insulting!

JOHN: Tell me what to say. Tell me and I'll say it!
I'll say whatever you want me to say!

DERRICK: I can't tell you what to say all the time.
How can we have a relationship if you
don't know what you do?

JOHN: Sometimes people just do things and they
don't think about it! I can't even remember
what happened ten minutes ago! Tell me
what I did, and I promise I won't do it
again!

Derrick turns.

DERRICK: *You cut me off!*

JOHN: I'm sorry I cut you off!

DERRICK: You're not.

JOHN: I am. I am. Look, look, if that's what I
      did—I'm sorry!

He turns and walks on. He chases after him.

DERRICK: You're making me crazy again!

John catches up and runs alongside Derrick.

JOHN: Okay, look—I remember, I remember—you
      were talking about the show and then I saw
      the dolphin and I got excited and I cut you
      off. I saw the dolphin, and that's all I saw. I
      blanked. You could've been saying anything
      to me.

DERRICK: Okay.

JOHN: You could've been telling me anything, and
      I couldn't've cared less.

DERRICK: Fine.

JOHN: All I wanted, right then and there, was to
      look at the dolphin. To show you the
      dolphin. It was like a white noise in my
      head!

DERRICK: Okay—enough.

Derrick stops.

DERRICK: This isn't working.

JOHN: Hey. Of course, it's working.

DERRICK: I knew—I knew this wouldn't work. We have too much history.

JOHN: History's a good thing. Where would we be without history? In caves!

DERRICK: I was enjoying being single again. Taking classes.

JOHN: You can still take classes.

DERRICK: Dating.

JOHN: You can still take classes.

DERRICK: We're just too different, John.

JOHN: We're not different.

DERRICK: You should be with some fun, frolicky guy. And I should be with someone I don't make crazy.

JOHN: I don't want someone fun and frolicky. I
      want you.

DERRICK: Okay.

JOHN: I'm sorry.

DERRICK: . . . okay.

JOHN: And . . . I'm listening.

Confession

M OM—I HAVE A CONFESSION TO MAKE."
"Okay."

"I'm not sure how to put this."

"Carrie. Just tell me. You know you can tell me anything."

"Okay. I—I'm—I've thought about this for a long time. And I've come to find that I am compatible with people of the opposite gender."

"I'm sorry. What?"

"I find that I am compatible with people of the opposite gender."

"You mean—you mean that—you like boys?"

"Well—that sounds creepy and weird when you put it like that. But basically, yes. I'm more interested—and attracted to—people of the opposite gender as me. Not all of them. But as a grouping classification on the whole, yes. That's right."

"Okay. I think I understand. Is that it?"

"That's it."

"So, is this new? I mean—were you going back and forth on this?"

"No."

"You weren't going back and forth?"

"Nope. Not at all."

"So, then you've always known you were straight?"

"Well, that's a weird word, isn't it? *Straight?* Like if I wasn't straight—I'm what? *Crooked?*"

"I mean—the point being that—this isn't a *new thing* for you?"

"No. I mean I didn't think about it at all when I was, like, what? Four? But basically—yes. I've always known that I was—"

"Normal?"

"Compatible with people of the opposite gender."

"Normal?"

"I would never put it that way."

"Maybe I'm just confused."

"By what?"

"Well—I didn't—I didn't ever think—or imagine that you *weren't* straight."

"Mom—"

"Normal."

"*Labels!*"

"I mean—maybe—maybe at some point I did. Sure. At some point, every parent worries. But you always had boyfriends. And not just as a—as a cover. So—"

"So?"

"So, I guess I just don't understand what you're confessing to, exactly."

"I just told you."

"I know, but—"

"I'm coming out to you."

"As straight?"

"*Oh my god!*"

"As 'compatible with the opposite gender'? Wow—that is a mouthful!"

"Yes."

"But—Carrie—*you don't need to do that.*"

"Why not?"

"It's assumed."

"By whom?"

"Whom what?"

"I don't know. I'm asking you."

"Who assumes it?"

"I don't know."

"*What?*"

"Third base!"

"You lost me."

"*Why is it assumed?*"

"Because—because it's—natural. It's normal. It's just naturally assumed that you're—perfectly fine. Normal."

"According to who?!"

"*Society.* Society. That's who. Jesus."

"Look. Let me ask you—if I felt compatible with *my own* gender, wouldn't you want me to tell you that? To confess that?"

"If you *were*—?"

"Say it."

"Gay."

"Yes."

"I—Sure. I mean—sure—I don't know. I guess so. If you felt like it. I mean—if I couldn't already figure it out for myself. Sure. But I've always been pretty goddamn sure that—"

"What if you weren't so sure about it? What if you didn't know—and it kept you up at night, worrying about it? Wouldn't you appreciate the clarity?"

"I don't know. I guess so. But that's not the situation—"

"Well, I'm clarifying it for you, anyway. That I feel compatible—"

"*With people of the opposite gender.* I get it. I get it."

"Great."

"Is that it?"

"Sure."

"Sure?"

"I thought having this conversation would give us—I don't know—a moment of understanding."

"Okay."

"And also, by having this conversation—this moment of understanding—I'm expressing solidarity with all of my friends who somehow currently feel the need to confess whatever stupid shit that they're currently confessing. I mean, if some people should feel compelled to confess, then why shouldn't *we all* confess? Or maybe we should all just confess that none of us really knows anything about ourselves."

"Carrie—"

"And honestly? The whole confession thing? I find abhorrent. Seriously. I don't know why anyone should have to confess to who they like or don't like. It's insane to me. So, I figured if one person should have to do it—then everyone should do it. So. So, that's why I'm telling you all of this."

"Carrie."

"What?"

"Who came out?"

"What?"

"Carrie . . ."

"It's not about—"

"*Carrie.*"

". . . Jason."

"Ah. Okay."

"That's not what this is about."

"Honey."

"It's *not* a big deal."

"Honey. Carrie. I'm so sorry."

"I just—I just—I just feel so—"

"I know."

"*Stupid.*"

"I know. I get it."

"God dammit."

"Honey. Carrie. You know that I would support anything you do."

"I know."

"Any decisions you would ever make in this regard."

"I know. I know. Thanks. Thank you."

"And sometimes life just fuckin' sneaks up on you."

"I know."

"And it's going to do that over and over and over. You
should get used to it."

"I know."

"Carrie."

"I know."

"I know you know."

"Thanks, Mom."

The Eight-Hour Kiss

A *LOVELY SUMMER EVENING IN THE EARLY 1960s. TWO AWKWARD*
teenagers, TIM and DEBBIE, both 16, sit next to each other
on a large couch on Debbie's front porch. There is a large clock hang-
ing near the front door which reads: 12 am (midnight). Light sounds
of the night—CRICKETS CHIRPING, an occasional
BULLFROG—can be heard. They look out at the stars.

TIM: Thanks for coming to the mixer with me
      tonight, Deb. It was sure a lot of fun.

DEBBIE: It sure was.

They sit awkwardly for a moment.

TIM: Great—great porch you've got here!

DEBBIE: Thanks.

They relax, slightly, and say nothing. We hear their thoughts
in VOICEOVER.

TIM (VO): Okay. Okay. I think—I think I can do this. I think—I could try—to—to—to actually—*kiss her.*

DEBBIE (VO): (*gazing at the stars*) Oh look—Saturn is at its greatest eastern elongation. How lovely.

TIM (VO): I'm just gonna . . . just gonna . . . reach over . . . here I go . . . nice and smooth—

He does nothing.

DEBBIE (VO): Probably no impact on the tides, though.

DEBBIE: Are you—are you comfortable?

TIM: Oh—oh sure! You?

DEBBIE: Uh huh.

TIM (VO): Nice and smooth—just put your arm around her . . . one . . . two . . . three . . .

He does nothing. BLACKOUT. Lights come back up. The large clock now reads: 1 am. Tim and Debbie are still frozen in the exact same spot.

TIM (VO): One . . . two . . . one . . . one . . . one . . . two . . . one . . . okay . . . okay . . .

TIM: I—I always did love all the sounds of the summer.

DEBBIE: Me, too.

The SOUNDS of the night grow louder. Debbie, in particular, listens.

TIM (VO): Okay—I'm gonna do it. Here we go.

He does nothing.

DEBBIE (VO): Say, that's the mating call of the *Rana catesbeiana*—or as we more commonly refer to it—the Canadian true bullfrog.

TIM (VO): I'm really gonna do it now! I really am!

DEBBIE (VO): Why—it's a complete chorus!

TIM (VO): Okay—I can do this—*I can do this! I can!* (beat) I can't do this! Why do I have to do it? Why can't she do it? This is the early 1960's! She could be assertive!

DEBBIE (VO): Alright. I guess I'd better take charge.

Debbie touches Tim's knee ever so slightly with her knee. Tim becomes aware of this. Debbie smiles to herself. Tim goes white, terrified. He doesn't move.

TIM (VO): Did—she just *touch my knee?!*

DEBBIE: (sighing) Ahhh . . .

TIM (VO): If she touched my knee, then that means . . . *something!*

DEBBIE (VO): He'd better not move his knee.

TIM (VO): I better not move my knee.

DEBBIE (VO): He'd better not move that knee.

TIM (VO): Is it moving? Is my knee moving? Did I just move it? Was that a movement?

A FLY buzzes around. They notice.

DEBBIE: Could you hand me that flyswatter?

Tim looks around for the swatter.

DEBBIE: It's over there.

She points to the ground, on Tim's side. He reaches for it. He can't reach it without moving his leg. He strains. He strains. He gets it. He gives it to her. She swats the fly quickly, efficiently. Tim perspires heavily.

DEBBIE: Got it.

BLACKOUT. Lights come back up. The large clock reads: 2 am. They are still frozen in the exact same spot.

TIM (VO): I can't feel my leg. I CAN'T FEEL MY LEG!

TIM stares at his leg. His leg starts nervously twitching. They both stare at it.

DEBBIE: You okay?

TIM: Sure.

DEBBIE: Tim—do you want a Coke?

TIM: Okay.

She reaches behind the couch, without barely moving, and withdraws two already opened cold Coke bottles from a cooler. She hands him a Coke.

TIM: Thanks.

DEBBIE: My pleasure.

TIM: You always keep a cooler of Cokes right
behind the ole couch, huh?

DEBBIE: For whenever company comes over.

Awkward long beat.

DEBBIE: Having fun?

TIM: Sure! You?

DEBBIE: Uh huh!

TIM: Great night!

DEBBIE: Sure is!

*They both continue sitting, quietly and frozen. She glances at
him, peripherally. He smiles, awkwardly.*

TIM (VO): Okay . . . Okay . . . here we go . . . here
we go . . .

*Finally, with full determination, Tim reaches over, slowly, cau-
tiously and extends his arm around Debbie. Debbie smiles and
puts her head on his shoulder. Tim smiles triumphant. (Beat.)*

Tim realizes that the arm around Debbie has the Coke in it. He stares at the Coke. The Coke stares at him. Debbie doesn't even notice. He forgets about it.

TIM (VO): Now—now, I definitely absolutely have to *kiss her.* That's the thing to do!

He does nothing.

BLACKOUT. Lights come back up. The large clock reads: 3 am. They are still frozen in the exact same spot. The Coke dangles from Tim's hand, spilling out.

TIM (VO): I'm gonna do it. I'm really really really really really really really gonna do it. I am. I mean it. Here we go. Here we go.

DEBBIE (VO): I think my shoulder's cramping.

TIM: It's—it's an awfully nice night.

DEBBIE: It sure is.

TIM (VO): God—it's so late! I should've been home hours ago! My parents will kill me!

DEBBIE (VO): Good thing my parents never check up on me. They're *so* progressive!

TIM (VO): I—I—I *have to do this!*

DEBBIE (VO): He'd better kiss me soon. I have to teach aqua aerobics in the morning.

BLACKOUT. Lights come back up. The large clock reads: 4 am. They are still frozen in the exact same spot. They're beginning to look exhausted.

DEBBIE (VO): Kiss me! Just kiss me! I have to go to sleep!

TIM (VO): Just . . . kiss . . . her . . . just . . . kiss . . . her . . . just . . . just . . . get it over with—

DEBBIE: I can't remember having such a wonderful evening.

TIM: Me neither.

DEBBIE (VO): You don't have to floss—you don't have to brush your teeth—just—

TIM (VO): I . . . I can do this!

DEBBIE (VO): Kiss me! *Jesus Christ! Just do it!*

TIM (VO): *Now!*

BLACKOUT. Lights come back up. The large clock reads: 5 am. They are still frozen in the exact same spot. Tim and Debbie now show serious signs of exhaustion.

TIM (VO): *Flintstones, meet the Flintstones—*

DEBBIE (VO): *They're creepy and they're kooky—*

TIM (VO): *They're the modern stone-age family—*

DEBBIE (VO): *Mysterious and spooky—*

TIM (VO): *From the town of bedrock—*

DEBBIE (VO): *They're all together ooky—*

DEBBIE: All good?

TIM: Yup.

TIM (VO): Oh God. Oh God. I've—I've been staring at her nose way too long.

DEBBIE (VO): Why can't I meet real men?

TIM (VO): Hello, Mr. Mole. Are you—are you a mole—or a beauty mark?

DEBBIE (VO): Why can't I meet real boys?

TIM (VO): You have two big hairs—and—and— are you cancerous, Mr. Mole?

DEBBIE (VO): He's never going to kiss me. If he
kisses me—I'll bet I throw up. If I
throw up, I wonder if he'll stop
kissing me? Nah.

TIM (VO): Okay—okay—getting a second wind.
I can do this. I—I—I—I—I—

BLACKOUT. *Lights come back up. The large clock reads: 6
am. They are still frozen in the exact same spot.*

TIM (VO): I hate her.

DEBBIE (VO): I hate him.

TIM (VO): Bitch!

DEBBIE (VO): Asshole!

DEBBIE: (*hyperactively*) *Nice night!*

TIM: (*hyperactively*) *Sure is!*

TIM (VO): I can't feel my arm!

DEBBIE (VO): I wish he'd move his fucking arm!

TIM (VO): *I'm sorry, Tim, but I'm afraid you're going to
lose that arm. I'm afraid we've got to amputate—*

Debbie subtly jabs her head against his arm several times, trying to hurt him. Tim doesn't even notice.

DEBBIE (VO): What are you—a masochistic? *Take a hint!*

TIM: Gettin' tired?!

DEBBIE: No, no—you?

TIM: Not at all!

DEBBIE (VO): *KISS ME OR GO HOME!*

BLACKOUT. Lights come back up. The large clock reads: 7 am. They are still frozen in the exact same spot. They look horrific. Huge dark rings under their eyes. Debbie slowly drifts asleep, while Tim keeps closing his eyes and then waking up, suddenly, with a start.

TIM (VO): Uh—uh—uh—uh—uh—uh—uh—uh— uh—uh—uh—uh—uh—uh—uh—uh— uh—

DEBBIE (VO): Uhhhhhhhhhhhhhhhhhhhhhhhhhhhh hhhhhhhhhhhhhhhhhhhhhhhhhhhh—

BLACKOUT. Lights come back up. The large clock reads:
8 am. They are still frozen in the exact same spot. They both
look like they're at death's door and fall in and out of stupor.
Tim blinks his eyes open. He looks at his watch and anx-
iously sees the time.

TIM: Uh . . . Debbie? Debbie? I gotta . . . I gotta go—

Debbie nods, semi-understanding.

DEBBIE: You do?

TIM: Uh . . . yeah . . .

DEBBIE (VO): Oh my gosh! He spent the whole
night here!

TIM (VO): I can't believe I stayed here the whole night.

TIM: Uhm . . . that was an awfully fun . . . something.

DEBBIE: Yeah—yes.

TIM: What are you doing tomorrow—I
mean—tonight?

DEBBIE: Tonight? Oh, I'm not sure.

TIM: Can I—call you?

DEBBIE: Uh . . . sure . . . okay . . .

With great pain and stiffness, he starts to get up. Debbie looks at him. Their eyes meet. He tenses and moves towards her in slow motion, their faces coming closer and closer together for a goodnight peck, but their faces collide in a full-on kiss. The kiss continues in a stiff lock, with neither having the energy to pull apart.

TIM (VO): So—tired.

DEBBIE (VO): So—tired.

TIM/DEBBIE (VO): *Can't—move!*

They remain frozen together, locked in their kiss.

A Clean Break

Early September 1996. Mid-day.

I'm driving down the I-40 W, just outside Knoxville, trying to quietly listen to the Allman Brothers. In the backseat Chloe blares The Breeders' *Cannonball* from the mini-speaker attached to her Walkman. Elle, near her, absently reads *People* magazine.

"Would you guys mind turning that down—"

"*Yes*," says Chloe. "*We mind.*"

"Uh," I say, "it's kind of distracting and hard to concentrate on the—"

"*Shut the fuck up, Milo!* You have one job here—*to drive*. That's it. So just shut the fuck up and *drive*. Do the one thing you seem mildly capable of without fucking it up."

"You don't have to be so hostile," I yell over the music.

"Excuse me?"

"You don't have to be so—"

"Don't fuckin' tell me how hostile or not hostile I should be. You're the last person on this planet that should be telling anyone how to fucking act."

Losing patience, I slow the car, and head towards the shoulder.

"*Don't you fucking pull over,*" says Chloe.

Nervously, I veer back to the highway, only slightly returning to the legal speed limit.

"You pull over again and I will climb up there and—"

"Chloe!" Elle finally interrupts. "*Enough!*"

Chloe turns and scowls out the window.

"Look," I say, "if we're going to do this together—can we at least try to be civil?"

A moment. Nothing. And then—Chloe explodes. She screams. She kicks repeatedly at the back of my seat.

"*Civil? Civil?!*" she yells.

I pull over to the shoulder. Chloe regards me, hatefully. Elle, unhappy, looks out the window at nothing.

"Look," I say. "I know—I know I've been a dick, but this is—fucking insane. If you can't control yourself—I'm happy to take you both to the nearest bus stop and let you figure out your own way home. Elle? Am I right? Is this not insane? I'm sorry, but I don't deserve this."

Chloe glares at me. I ignore her.

"*Elle?*"

Elle steels herself and looks at me—a wave of restrained hurt across her face.

"Can you give us a minute?" she says.

I get out of the car, taking the keys with me, and sit on the front hood in the hot, baking sun. I hear them in the back seat, whispering. Chloe is pissed, but now so is Elle. I look back and see Chloe, stewing, turn and stare out the window.

"*Fine,*" she says. "*Fine. Whatever.*"

Elle, Chloe, and I had been on the road for two days now. The trip wasn't supposed to be like this. The trip, originally, was supposed to be just Elle and me, blissfully, happily traveling west to our new home, where eventually we'd marry and settle down and raise kids.

But of course, all of that changed when I broke up with her.

Elle and I had been dating steadily and were fairly inseparable for the previous two years. We did everything together. We had the same sense of humor, loved the same food, music, drugs. Finished each other's sentences. We were so goddamn cute together that most of our friends wanted nothing to do with us.

We had made plans to move to Los Angeles earlier in the year. Ozzie—one of my best friends from college—had a sure-fire job opportunity waiting for me at his production company, and he knew about some decent, affordable housing near him. He could help set Elle and I up, no problem. It was going to be a whole new incredible life.

With the big move looming, Elle and I spent the summer apart. She gave up her Chelsea apartment and crap retail job to do a summer advertising internship in Chicago, while I remained at Murray Hill working short-term data entry jobs and getting production assistant gigs whenever I could. Over the summer I would secure a car for us, and then, in September, we'd meet back up and road trip out west.

However, when Elle returned to New York a weird thing happened. I started having panic attacks. Anxiety. I couldn't sleep at night. The traffic and street noises that were usually just white noise to me were now deafening. I was feeling constant, intense claustrophobia. It wasn't something I could explain verbally. I just knew, somehow, I couldn't move out west with her.

So, I told her, and it was abrupt and devastating. I told her that I was incredibly, incredibly sorry. She was stunned, hurt, shocked, overwhelmed. She had quit her job, given up her apartment, uprooted her entire life to move out to Los Angeles with me and now I'd ruined everything.

"You quit your job to take the Chicago internship," I reminded her, hopefully.

"I took the internship because I thought we were leaving New York."

💔

Our break-up didn't just piss Elle off, it also pissed off all of her friends—*"our" friends*—none more so than excitable, manic Chloe with her ever-changing patch of dyed hair (this week, pink). To Chloe, this was the greatest betrayal imaginable and she hated me for it. *Hated me. Detested me.* And so, it was her idea that, at the very least, I owed Elle a full trip from New York to Los Angeles—and any other weird, roadside Americana stops in between.

Traveling alone with me, however, would be unbearable for Elle. So, Chloe would come along as our chaperone. I would drive the two of them across the country, then shortly after arriving in LA, they'd catch a flight back to New York.

That was the new plan.

So, I said "fine." A quick trip west and then a clean break. What could go wrong?

The first day was tense and dull but straightforward. We had quickly reviewed the map and stops along the way and I asked if there was anywhere in particular that they wanted to go.

"We'll let you know," said Chloe, tersely.

They had made it clear to me: this was not a social trip. I was their driver and my job was to keep to myself and safely get them across the country. Period. I sat alone up front, driving, while they sat together in the back. They read books and magazines, listened to their Walkmans, stared out the windows. Initially, they hardly even spoke to each other, much less to me. I knew better than to engage them and listened to the radio—tuned to play only in the front of the car—and kept my eyes on the road.

On the first afternoon, we stopped briefly at a rest area for gas and lunch. When I got my food and came over to sit with them, they both quickly got up and moved to a different table.

By the end of our long first day, we finally arrived at a motel.

"Rooms?" said the manager.

"Two," said Chloe.

"Hold on a sec," I said, taking them aside. "We don't have enough money for two rooms every night."

We had almost no money. At best maybe $600 between the three of us for gas, food, and motel rooms for the week and that was it. We all had had shit jobs back in New York. Chloe worked at a non-profit and made even less than I did at my data entry jobs. For myself, I had saved up exactly enough money just to get to LA and Ozzie's.

"That's not our problem," said Chloe.

"Do the rooms have two beds?" I asked the manager.

"Sure."

"What kind?"

"Queens."

"Perfect."

So, we got a single room with two queens. We brought our luggage inside and settled in.

After about an hour, Chloe said to me, "could you get us some ice?"

I went to get ice. When I got back, the door was locked. And in front of it was a blanket, pillow, and my car keys.

"*Elle! Chloe!*" I banged on the door. "*This isn't funny! Elle!*"

They ignored me. Other guests peered out of their windows at me—*who the hell is doing all this yelling?*

I went back to the manager's office, but it was locked, with a sign reading: "Hours of operation—8a–10p. Have a nice day!"

So, I slept in the backseat of my car for the first night of our trip.

And the second night.

And the third night.

By night three, I had become resigned to sleeping in the car. On night three, no one pulled any tricks on me or locked me out, I simply walked into the motel room, grabbed a blanket and pillow, and got into my car. It was sad and uncomfortable, but I had come to appreciate the silence and alone-time. When rumbling, honking trucks weren't pulling in and out—I dozed fractiously.

By day four, intensely sleep-deprived, I started falling asleep at the wheel, and weaved in and out of traffic. Had I been with true loved ones, I would've asked for help. But exhaustion, depression, and disassociation had given me tunnel vision, and I kind of just didn't care anymore.

"*Milo! Milo!*" came the super loud screaming from the back seat. "*Jesus Christ! Pull the fuck over!*"

Half brain-dead, I pulled onto the shoulder and slumped over. I faintly heard them get out of the back of the car, open my door, haul me out of the front seat, dump me into the backseat, and then drive off. The bumps and the rattling weren't great on my stomach, but the heat and vibrations of the moving car lulled me.

Several hours later.

"Milo? We're here," said someone.

"Where's here?" I rasped, shielding my eyes from the brilliant, hot sun. I heard them get out of the car. We were in some giant, empty field, shaded by a massive billboard with a cartoon picture of an immense redneck trucker on it with a gigantic Rambo-like rifle in his hands. Deep in the distance was the sound of explosions.

"What's going on?" I asked.

"We're here to shoot guns," said Elle.

They left and I stayed in the car for another hour or so, falling in and out of sleep.

CRACK! CRACK CRACK! went the abrupt discharge of gunfire.

I found myself dreaming that I was accompanying Martin Sheen in his quest for Captain Kurtz in *Apocalypse Now*—which, in a way, seemed more relaxing than this trip.

CRACK! CRACK!

and then

AKAKAKAKAKAKAKAKAK!

as if someone had discovered automatic weapons.

💔

Suddenly I urgently had to go to the bathroom. I got the back car door open, stumbled out of the car and immediately threw up. After collecting myself, I staggered over to a large, dirt-colored concrete warehouse with a gigantic sign BIG ED'S AMMO SHACK!

Inside were more guns, knives, rifles, hanging canoes, stuffed bears, elk, bison, and every-everything camouflage than I'd ever seen in my life. Four or five huge, stocky guys with immense beards and flannel shirts with the sleeves poorly ripped off wandered around helping customers. One impressively tough-looking guy with a mullet and half a dozen earrings in his left ear presented a large hand-gun to Chloe and Elle. Elle looked bored, but Chloe was in seventh heaven. The guy, who looked like he couldn't decide if he wanted to be a farmer or a pirate, flirted energetically with Chloe and showed her how to aim the gun.

"Are we almost done here?" I asked as passive-aggressively as I could muster.

"I may buy a gun," said Chloe, enthusiastically.

"Don't you need a license for that?"

"Do it all right here," said the Farmer-Pirate.

I looked at the price-tag stickered to the gun. It was in the thousands.

"I think you need the dollar-store version, Chloe," I said.

"Do total financing right here," said the Pirate-Farmer.

I leaned towards Elle.

"Can we please just get out of here?" I asked.

"Not till after the party," said Chloe, smugly.

"Heathcliff's brother is having a party, a couple miles down the road," said Elle.

"Heathcliff?" I said, looking at the Farmer-Pirate.

Elle nodded.

"Big Ed's his brother."

I noticed a giant sign hanging from the ceiling that said, BIG ED'S AMMO SHACK—BIGGEST AND BEST OUTDOOR SUPPLY OUTLET IN ABILENE!

Abilene?

"Where exactly are we?" I asked Elle.

"We're in Hawley, just outside of Abilene," said Elle.

"We're still in Texas," Chloe grinned at me, evilly.

"We're supposed to be in New Mexico," I said. "We needed to be in New Mexico today. That was the program."

"New Mexico don't have no place like Big Ed's," said Heathcliff.

"We don't need an ammo shack," I said. "We need to be in Albuquerque."

I headed towards the exit, a man with a goal, but heard a familiar jangling sound. I turned and saw Chloe dangling my car keys.

"*After the party*," she said.

💔

Big Ed's party was a blowout, crowded with bikers, hellraisers, and a mob of folks who looked like extras from *Roadhouse*. Both Chloe and Elle danced with hirsute, oversized locals, and I imagined some scenario where I was expected to bravely go up against one of these guys and then get my ass kicked all over the lawn. But hell, if they wanted to dance *or anything* with anyone there, what business was it of mine? Besides, I'd gotten a glimpse of Elle and she looked miserable. Eventually, I just went back to the car and recuperated.

By 10 p.m., hungry, I made my way into the house's kitchen and found a broad-shouldered woman basting a large roast chicken. She smiled at me with perhaps the most normal, friendliest smile I'd seen in a week.

"Could I—could I use your phone, please?" I asked.

"'Course," she said.

"It's a call to Los Angeles. So, I don't know if—"

I reached into my pocket for some loose cash to offer her.

"Please," she said. "It's fine."

"Thanks," I said. "Thanks so much."

A minute later, I had Ozzie on the phone.

"We're going to be a day or so late," I said. "No—we took a—it's a long story. I'm in Hawley, Texas. We're fine. Chloe and Elle are both here. It's—yeah. Elle and I—we broke up, Ozzie. Yeah. They just came for the trip. Then they're flying back east after a couple days. Yeah. Thanks. I'll call when I get in. Thanks. I appreciate it, Oz. Thank you. Talk to you."

I hung up.

"Broke up with the one out there with Heath?" asked the woman, as she basted the chicken.

"No, no—I—the other one."

"Oh," said the woman. "Other one seems sweet."

"Yes," I said. "She is."

"Want some chicken?" asked the woman.

"Yes, please. Thanks."

She cut off a few pieces and put them on a plate in front of me. At that moment, I ate the best chicken I'd ever tasted in my life. She sat with me and watched me eat.

"They makin' your life hell on this trip?"

"Yes," I said, "but I probably deserve it."

"Probably," she said. "Sounds temporary at any rate."

"I hope so," I said. "I'm Milo, by the way."

"Nancy," she said, wiping her hand off with a towel and then shaking mine.

"Nice to meet you," I said. "So, you're—"

"Heathcliff's wife," said Nancy.

"Ah," I said.

Then Elle came into the kitchen.

"Is there any more food?" she asked.

Nancy set her up with a plate and then left the room. Elle ate, and then looked at me, wide-eyed.

"This is *really* good," she said.

"It's like the best chicken I've ever had in my life," I said.

"I'm sorry about Chloe," said Elle. "This whole trip was a mistake."

"No, no, I'm sorry," I said. "I'm sorry I put you in this position. I just—I don't know what I was thinking."

"It's okay," said Elle, annoyed, picking at her food.

"No, it's not," I said. "I know I fucked up your whole life, Elle. I didn't mean to. I just . . . I realized that I have no idea what's going to happen out there—I don't know anybody but Ozzie. And you know how unreliable he is. I don't know what this job's going to be, but it's probably going to be pretty shitty and pay terribly."

"I know," said Elle.

"It's hard enough that I decided to make my own life super shitty. And I realized I was about to make your life super-shitty, too."

"So, you dumped me."

"Well, I wasn't thinking of it like that—I was thinking that I was *freeing* you."

"I didn't asked to be freed," she said. "I chose to go with you. My eyes were wide open."

"Well, anyway, I'm sorry."

"You should be."

"It's probably going to suck in LA, Elle."

"It doesn't matter anymore, Milo. And anyway—it is going to suck in LA. More than you think."

I looked at her, strangely.

"Ozzie doesn't have a job waiting for you," she said.

"Excuse me?"

"He doesn't have a job for you. He told me that the morning we left. He told me when he first heard that we'd broken up."

"I didn't know you talked to him."

"I know you didn't."

"Fuck."

"Yeah."

"What a fucking asshole."

"Yup."

"You're not bullshitting me?"

I stared at her, stunned.

"Son-of-a-bitch. I just got off the phone with him. I told him we were running late, and he said don't worry about it. What an unbelievable asshole."

"Yeah. We're running late to nothing."

"Fuck. And—Chloe knows all this, too."

"Sure. She loves that you didn't know. That you thought you were heading to a big job. It was supposed to be a huge joke on you."

"*Fuck.*"

"Yeah. She wanted me not to tell you."

She stared at her stripped off chicken bones.

"Thanks for telling me."

She sighed, and I knew she was thinking, *it doesn't even matter anymore.*

After that night, the trip became . . . less eventful. Less stressful. Chloe was less hostile to me and the two of them began speaking to me, occasionally. They still stayed in the back of the car, but now they were open to playing road trip games—Twenty Questions, naming countries that started and ended with consecutive letters, travel bingo, and so on. On the fifth night, when I grabbed my blanket and pillow from the motel room and got in the car, I soon heard the two of them tapping on the glass, waking me to come inside and sleep in the unoccupied bed. I slept ten hours that night—the longest, deepest sleep I'd had in weeks.

We had short, tolerable visits to the Grand Canyon and Vegas. Eventually, we got to Los Angeles. We met up with Ozzie for an awkward half hour at a diner. And by the time we met him, he knew I knew he was full of shit about all of our plans together.

So.

After all of this, I ended up staying in LA for three years. I only saw Ozzie twice after that first day, both times by accident. After that first awkward half hour, our friendship was essentially over.

It was worse than that, actually. About seven months later, I heard an uglier truth—that Ozzie had initially hoped to coerce both Elle and I to stay in LA in hopes that she would dump me, whereupon he would "swoop in on her." Ozzie had always had a thing for Elle.

I had cobbled this story about Ozzie's intentions from reports from three different friends, and, in retrospect, it didn't seem so unbelievable.

I lived on various people's couches in Los Angeles for about two-and-a-half months total before I found steady production assistant work and a place I could afford.

Generally, life there was about as spirit-crushing as I'd imagined it would be. But I grit my teeth and got the production and crew experience that I had so desperately wanted, and by the time I made my way back to New York, I had a fairly usable resume.

Surprisingly, Chloe, Elle, and I remained together for the rest of their few days in Los Angeles. We decamped at Chloe's dementia-ridden grandfather Nestor's apartment in San Marino. He was in his late eighties and had people who came in to assist him twice a day. He didn't quite recognize Chloe, but he seemed to enjoy having the company. Chloe and Elle stayed in his extra room, while I curled up on an open area of the carpet in the living room near his old piano. (The couch was a possibility, but it was inch deep in cat hair. Did I mention he had cats? He had six cats.)

For those last few days, the three of us were very touristy. We went to the Hollywood sign and Venice Beach and Disneyland. Disneyland was our big final destination and the one time on that trip that we all actually laughed together.

By the time we got to the entrance of the happiest place on earth, we had all lost tremendous weight, and were emotionally and physically drained. We each looked like if someone just slightly grazed us, we would collapse into ourselves.

As we stood tiredly looking at the giant, happy Mickey Mouse topiary clock carved into the front entranceway, Chloe started laughing manically, uncontrollably.

"*We fuckin' made it to Disneyland!*" she said.

"We fuckin' made it to Disneyland," said Elle.

"We fuckin' made it to Disneyland," I agreed.

Exactly then, the tiniest, most inoffensively dressed, most touristy woman I'd ever seen, in tiny pink pastel shorts, and with deep blue varicose veins, came over and said, sweetly, "would you like me to take y'all's picture?"

And the three of us burst out laughing.

"That would be fuckin' brilliant," said Chloe, handing her camera to the woman.

The woman generously took our picture.

I finally saw that picture some ten years later at a college reunion. Elle's husband was there, as was Chloe's partner. We drank and didn't hate each other. Chloe pulled out that picture and now, you almost wouldn't recognize us. There we were, the three of us at Disneyland—thin, dirty, ratty—and laughing hysterically, like we were truly enjoying each other's company and having the time of our lives.

Sexpo 2041

*T*HE YEAR *2041. A* FUTURISTIC SUBURBAN LIVING ROOM, *very space-agey, but domestic. DON, looking approximately mid-fifties, rushes around packing things into compact, futuristic suitcases. He swipes through images on a tablet.*

DON: Peg?! Peggy! The shuttle's gonna be here any minute, hon'!

He feels a buzzing in his pocket, checks a miniature phone device.

DON: (*into the phone*) Hello? Yes? They'll be waiting at the hotel? Great! Thank you so much! (*calling offstage*) Honey! Come on!

He examines himself in the phone, preens.

DON: Don-baby, you're lookin' very very good for a man your age!

He makes several swipes on his tablet and taps a schedule. PEG—looking approximately mid-fifties—enters. She sits on the couch.

DON: Hey, hon—the shuttle's gonna be here any minute. Y'know, when you asked me to plan our events, I thought I was going to hate it. But I gotta tell you, I am surprisingly great at this! I just got us into *Synchronized Sex*, the *Antigrav Orgy* on Thursday, and—*and!*—I actually got us into the *Sexual Congress!* With six other states! Not bad!

PEG: (*non-plussed*) That's great, Don.

DON: Oh! And later tonight—*Speed Sex!*

PEG: You won that last year.

DON: Unintentionally! But yeah—I've still got my medal!

Peg says nothing. Don continues to race around, grabbing items to pack, enthusiastically.

DON: Y'know if we hurry—

PEG: Don—

DON: We can still probably get into—

PEG: Don. (*beat*) I've decided not to go.

DON: (*confused*) I'm—I'm sorry—what?

PEG: I've decided not to go. To *Sexpo*.

DON: What do you mean you've decided not to
        go? Of course, we're going.

PEG: I'm being serious. I've—I've decided I'm not
        going to go to *Sexpo*. But that's just me. You
        should still go.

Don's phone buzzes. He answers.

DON: (*into phone*) Hi. We're—I'm sorry—(*to Peggy*)
        See?! Now, we're running late! (*into phone*)
        No, I'm sorry. We'll catch the next one.
        Thank you. (*hangs up, addresses Peggy*) What
        are you talking about?

PEG: I know this is important to you and—I know
        you're very excited to go have sex with a lot
        of other people. And I respect that.

DON: I don't just want to have sex with other people.
        I want to have sex with other people—*and you*.

PEG: I don't know how to explain this. It's too—too—

DON: It's too much? Okay. Got it. Gotten. (*looks at his tablet*) Look. There's plenty here to trim. *Naked hang gliding, speed sex*—okay, okay—is that enough? Fine. Fine. I hate to cut all this but—*Boom! Wild animal safari!* Cut! They're all gone. I just cut a quarter of our schedule! Okay? See how flexible I am?! And—and that actually frees us up to—

PEG: Don. It's not about cutting events. It's—it's the whole trip. I can't do it.

DON: Peg—you can't just say at the last minute that you don't want to go! We can't *not* go. We've got tickets to a dozen fucking events! *Literally! Fucking events!*

PEG: Don—

DON: We made plans, Peggy. With Roger and Felicia and Julian and Mikhaela and Ross and Adam and Bailey and—and—someone named Carter. And I have my high school reunion— which—

PEG: You're really looking forward to.

DON: Yes, I am. I haven't seen those folks—

PEG: Naked—

DON: In years! Yes! (*beat*) Look—Peggy, what is it?
Is it the sex with strangers?

PEG: No.

DON: With friends?

PEG: No.

DON: With large groups? Small groups? Different
species? Is it the probes? You used to like the
probes!

PEG: I did like the probes. It's not the probes.

DON: The anti-grav sex makes you nauseous?

PEG: It does. But that's not it. (*beat*) I just—I can't.

DON: Because?

PEG: Because I have a ticket—to somewhere else.

Long beat. Don is stunned.

DON: *Somewhere else?*

PEG: Yes.

DON: Where?

PEG: *Etera—*

DON: *The glacier planet?!*

PEG: Yes.

DON: You want to skip *Sexpo* to go to the goddamn glacier planet?!

PEG: Yes.

DON: To do what?!

PEG: To go hiking.

DON: *Hiking*?! (*incredulous*) You can't be serious!?

PEG: I am.

DON: You want us to skip *Sexpo*—during a *Sex
Olympics year*—to go *hiking*?!

Beat.

PEG: I didn't say "us."

He stares at her.

DON: Okay. So, it's me. So, you're sick of me?!

PEG: No. No. Not at all. I'm just—I'm tired, Don.

DON: Of me.

PEG: No. Stop saying that. Stop making this about *you*. I just—I need to slow things down now. For myself. To collect myself.

DON: And you already had this ticket? The entire time I was planning this trip. You knew I was killing myself planning this trip—when all the while you had a ticket somewhere else?! (*beat*) Did you *ever* intend to go to *Sexpo*?

PEG: I don't know. Yes. At first, I thought I did want to go. And then—I didn't. But I didn't want to spoil your plans.

DON: So—without telling me about it—you bought a ticket for a *completely different trip?!*

PEG: Yes. It was—it was actually kind of rash. Exciting. Frivolous.

DON: *Sexpo is rash, exciting and frivolous! That's basically all it is!*

PEG: Don—please—you do what you need to do. And I'll do what I need to do.

DON: This is a break-up. After sixty years. You're breaking up with me.

PEG: That's not what this is.

DON: And I'm supposed to—what? Drop *Sexpo*
　　　and go hiking with you?

PEG: You won't want to.

DON: (*firmly*) As always, I want to do whatever
　　　you're doing. (*beat*) *What exactly are you doing?*

She pulls out a tablet, flips through it.

PEG: Well, first I'm going to go on an incredibly
　　　long hike. About eleven miles.

DON: Yes.

PEG: And then . . . I may read a book.

DON: And?

PEG: That's it. (*beat*) I told you this was not your
　　　kind of trip. You'd be miserable. And honestly,
　　　I don't want someone miserable on my trip.

DON: Oh, you hate it when someone ruins your trip?

PEG: Yes.

DON: 'Cause that's how I feel. (*beat*) So, let me get
　　　this straight—if I go to *Sexpo without you*, I'll
　　　be miserable. And if I go hiking *with you*, I'll
　　　be miserable. Either way I'm miserable.

PEG: Don—

DON: Peggy—I feel that we are somehow experienc-
ing meltdown here. I feel that our relationship
is suddenly—after sixty years—somehow
crashing down around us, and that you're
utterly utterly rejecting me, that you're abandoning the very notion of our relationship.

PEG: Well, maybe the notion was—

DON: What?

PEG: Wrong.

DON: *Wrong?*

PEG: People change, Don.

DON: Really? Really? I haven't changed! Have you
changed? How exactly have you changed,
Peg? Have you seen yourself lately—?

PEG: Don—

He holds up his phone and shows her her reflection.

DON: Is this really the face of a—God, I don't even
know how old you are anymore—91? 92? 93?
How old are you, Peg?

PEG: 93.

DON: 93! Who would know, Peg?! With all the
upgrades and micro-cosmetics and continuous
replacement parts for what—*twenty-five years
now?!* No one has changed less than you, Peg.

PEG: Actually—actually—I have made a change.

DON: Oh yeah? What?

PEG: The upgrading. The cosmetics. The body
parts.(*beat*) I stopped. (*beat*) Several months ago.

Long beat. He stares at her, unsure of what she's saying.

DON: I'm sorry. You did what?

PEG: I stopped—

DON: I heard you. Don't make jokes like that.

PEG: I'm not making a joke.

DON: (*flipping through screens on his tablet*) You *have*
been replacing parts. I know you've been
replacing parts—I've got monthly bills. I've
seen them. We've been—

PEG: They were visits. Checkups. I know you don't
look at the records that closely. I haven't
gotten anything new in more than—

DON: How long?

PEG: Eight months.

Long beat.

DON: (*furious*) *Are you out of your mind?!* (*beat*) You
     can't do that! You can't just—

PEG: I know.

DON: *You can't just stop.*

PEG: I know.

DON: It doesn't work that way!

PEG: I know.

DON: You can't just cut yourself off without—

PEG: I—

DON: *Stop saying 'I know'!* (*pulling out his cellphone*)
     We need to get you an appointment right
     now! Forget *Sexpo* and hiking—you have to
     go back and change this—*right now!*

PEG: Don—

*Don paces, glued to his cellphone. He checks the number, calls
again.*

DON: *Goddammit!!* No one's answering! *He's
  probably at Sexpo! Goddammit!*

PEG: Don, I made my choice—

DON: Peggy—hold on—

She takes his hand, looks into his eyes.

PEG: Don. It's done.

Don puts away the phone. He pulls away from her.

DON: Goddammit, Peggy! (*beat*) *You'll age.*

PEG: I know.

DON: *Rapidly.*

PEG: I know.

Long beat.

DON: *You'll die.*

PEG: We all do. (*beat*) I—

DON: *No! No!* This was not your decision to make! This
  is supposed to be a decision we make together! You

did this—without telling me anything! That is not fair to me, Peggy. This is completely utterly unfair! (*beat*) If I'd done exactly the same thing to you—

PEG: I would have never let you do it.

DON: That's right!

PEG: Which is why I didn't tell you. Until now. Until—until—

DON: It was too late.

PEG: Yes.

DON: Until it was irreversible?

PEG: Yes.

Long beat.

DON: That's not fair to me, Peggy. That's not how this works.

PEG: I know, Don. I know. I struggled with telling you—and I didn't because I knew you would talk me out of it. You absolutely would have. And I didn't want to be talked out of it. This was the right thing for me, Don. I had to do this. I had to. You have every right to be angry—

DON: You've killed yourself.

PEG: It's not like that. I talked to the doctor. It won't be—drastic. It will be—

DON: What?

PEG: Normal.

DON: Normal?

PEG: Proper. It may even be—graceful.

DON: Fuck proper and graceful. (*beat*) Peggy— please—please try to get this reversed. Call the doctor. Get back on the program.

PEG: Because I can?

DON: Because I want you to. Because I love you. Please.

PEG: I can't do it.

Long beat.

PEG: I can't do this anymore, Don. I can't. This isn't who I am. On the inside. I've been dying on the inside for years now. I want to let go. You have to help me let go. I'm just so tired.

Long beat. Don swipes several screens on his tablet. He lets the tablet fall to the ground.

DON: It's done. The whole trip. Gone. Canceled. Expunged. Goodbye *Sexpo*. (*beat*) How long do we even have, Peg?

PEG: We have time. Probably . . . a few years.

DON: While you age and wither and wrinkle and—

PEG: And you don't.

DON: You're getting the better end of the deal.

She smiles.

PEG: I probably am. (*beat*) Don—why don't you come hiking with me? (*beat*) We can hike and read books. And you can watch me wither and age and wrinkle. (*beat*) And we can stroll in the woods and fish and swim. And stay up late by the light of a fire. (*beat*) And you can make love to an old woman under the stars. (*beat*) And we can talk.

Long beat.

DON: When do we leave?

Toilet Paper
& Kleenex

*T*HE STAGE IS SET TO RESEMBLE A GIGANTIC, FAIRLY CLEAN *and tidy bathroom. TOILET PAPER and KLEENEX stand not too far from each other—stuck in their respective areas—and converse with one another and also the audience. Kleenex has the air of a somewhat gentile lady. Toilet Paper is slightly more brutish and may have a Cockney accent.*

KLEENEX: (*to audience*) I'm Kleenex.

TOILET PAPER: (*to audience*) And I'm Toilet Paper.

KLEENEX: We're both tissues. I'm the classier tissue. Elite. Special. Reserved for that most precious of areas—the face—and, as necessary—the nostrils!

TOILET PAPER: I'm used on the bum. Nether regions. Downtown. I'm cheap, too. Thirty rolls for ten.

KLEENEX: My world is orderly, immaculate. Everything in its place.

TOILET PAPER: I sit on a roll and spin. Not that I'm complaining.

KLEENEX: After use, I'm gently crumpled.

TOILET PAPER: I'm flushed. All day long. Flush, flush, flush.

KLEENEX: (*proudly*) People never flush Kleenex!

TOILET PAPER: (*incredulous*) Suuuure, they don't.

HANDKERCHIEF enters and stands near them. He is aristocratic, perfect, almost an angel. Kleenex and Toilet Paper stare at him, stunned.

HANDKERCHIEF: (*to TP & K*) Hello!

KLEENEX: My goodness! Who are you?!

HANDKERCHIEF: I'm handkerchief!

KLEENEX/TOILET PAPER: Ooooh!

TOILET PAPER: I've heard of you.

HANDKERCHIEF: Must've gotten lost on the way to the laundry! Excuse me—dry cleaner! What a lovely place you have!

KLEENEX: It's our home.

HANDKERCHIEF: Love the tile.

KLEENEX: Are you a tissue?

HANDKERCHIEF: Ha, ha, ha! Heavens, no! I'm what they call a *linen!* Live in the master's bedroom. Top shelf bureau—and folded *quite* neatly! I'm only used on fancy occasions. Then, afterwards— I'm cleaned, *chemically!*

KLEENEX/TOILET PAPER: *Ahhh . . .*

KLEENEX: They re-use you?!

HANDKERCHIEF: 'Course! Then I'm all fresh and new again. I'm only used at the fanciest of affairs!

TOILET PAPER: (*burping loudly*) I'm two-ply.

KLEENEX: I'd love to go to a dry cleaner . . .

HANDKERCHIEF: Well, I don't think that'd
                           work so well! You'd burn up!

Kleenex, gasps, horrified, and starts to cry.

KLEENEX: Burn up?!

TOILET PAPER: That's an awful thing to say!

HANDKERCHIEF: Well, it's true!

TOILET PAPER: (*to Kleenex*) There now! Stop
                           that! You'll shrivel . . . !

A BOY'S VOICE shouts from OFFSTAGE.

BOY (OS): Mom! The dog's peed again!

MOM (OS): Well, clean it up!

BOY (OS): Toilet paper or Kleenex?

MOM (OS): No—no! Use a rag!

BOY (OS): Oh, here's one!

*A GIGANTIC HAND reaches in and grabs Handkerchief
and abruptly pulls him backwards off the stage.*

HANDKERCHIEF: Rag?! I'm not a—NOOOO!!

Sound of HANDKERCHIEF SCREAMING offstage.

BOY (OS): Aw! That was way too flimsy! I'll grab towels!

Sound of a door opening, offstage and then the VOICES OF TOWELS, SCREAMING.

TOWELS (OS): NO! NO! EUWWWWWW!!!

Toilet Paper and Kleenex take deep breaths, shocked.

BOY (OS): (*happily*) That worked!

The SOUNDS die out and Toilet Paper and Kleenex are left in silence again.

TOILET PAPER: That was horrible.

Beat.

KLEENEX: Toilet paper?

TOILET PAPER: Yeah?

KLEENEX: Y'know, we're not so different, really.
We're basically the same thing in
different packaging. (*beat*) Except I
have aloe.

TOILET PAPER: Mmm.

KLEENEX: I mean—it's not so bad, is it?

TOILET PAPER: Not at all. Why, I get to sit and
spin all day. Who could ask for
more?

KLEENEX: And I get to sit right by the mirror.

Beat. They look at each other.

TOILET PAPER & KLEENEX: With you.

Album

I'M WITNESSING A MIRACLE OF MODERN SCIENCE. WELL, okay, it's not that modern. The only real modern thing is the room we're in—the entire maternity wing, actually—recently redesigned to look/feel like a posh hotel, like the Ritz. This room itself is actually bigger than our first apartment—and way better furnished. But what I'm witnessing is as old as the Earth itself:

The birth of my son.

♥

I'm leaning against my stove. I'm wearing jeans. I'm in my socks. It's cold outside, mid-January. My prospective roommate looks around the room. She wears a too-hip black leather jacket, black scarf and Doc Martens and sports a bobbed, late-eighties haircut. She's cute, seems friendly, just one more in a parade of potential roommates.

I'm blasé. What else could I be? The whole thing is annoy-ing. I can't afford the rent by myself. I could probably skate by, but I'd rather have the money. And I'm used to having a roommate. Besides this tiny, crumbling piece of shit is prime Manhattan real estate, right? I won't downright screw any-body. But sure, I'll take the bigger room—let the new roomie pick up the bulk of rent. Why not? It's my apartment.

A parade of potential housemates descends on me: art-ists, students, freshly minted temp workers.

I call the service. Look, I say, I specifically said *no women*. No women, no pets, no smokers. The apartment's small enough as it is. I need someone quiet, easy-going. No tension.

Oh, oh—our mistake, they say. We'll change the form. Sorry. Uhm—there are going to be some women coming by—could you please just be *nice* to them. They're paying a fee, y'know. Sorry.

Nice? Hhhn. No, no—I tell the next woman. This was a mistake.

Mistake?! I paid $125 for this list.

$125? Really? To look at my place? I'm *so* sorry. Okay, so I'll pretend—sure, I might take a female roommate. Mm. Well, look, maybe I could take a female roommate. I'm easy-going, flexible. I've had gay roommates. How bad could a woman be? I'm not looking to get laid. I'm an adult. I'm looking for another human being to share an incredibly small amount of space with: gay, straight, black, white, female, male. It doesn't matter. If it's right, it's right. Just gimme a year till the lease is up.

She's casual, low-key, friendly. She looks around. It's small, but how much room does she really need? No one spends time in a Manhattan apartment. The rent's not too bad. And for work—she's doing something—some medical thing. Good. No actors, no artists. Medicine can pay the rent. The small talk is about as good as small talk gets. At one point, she turns and—*shit, she broke my lamp.*

Sorry!

No, no, it's okay—

Lamp? It's a pole with a shade held on by a pencil. A broken pencil. She's looking for a year. Great.

I'll probably never see her again.

My wife is having a baby. My baby.

I'm telling Bill I don't know what's happening to me. I'm trying to be calm—to be normal. Adult. But it feels—it feels like it's getting more involved. Intense. The apartment is so small. I don't want it to get weird. I don't want to do the wrong thing. I don't even know what the wrong thing is. I don't know. We're spending an incredible amount of time together. Not unnaturally—nothing forced. We're just—that's what we're doing. Going to shops in the Village. I helped her buy some bookshelves and we carried them all the way back to the apartment—ten or eleven blocks over and up three flights of stairs. I don't know. She's smart, passionate. The apartment's so small. I don't want to be a scumbag or anything. I don't—I don't know what I'm thinking.

But I like her.

I'm on a John Wayne kick. I've got to see every John Wayne movie ever made. I just read an article about "The Conqueror." John Wayne plays Genghis Khan leading an army of Huns. It's supposed to be one of the worst films ever made—not just because it's purely bad—but because it was filmed on a former A-bomb test site which eventually killed Wayne, his co-stars, and several crewmen via cancer. But it's unintentionally hysterically funny, highlighted by the moving love story of Khan, formerly known as "Temujin," and his Hun gal, Bortai. We stay up late into the night watching and talk about it for days afterward.

At a concert. We're all here as friends. I'm here and she's here and her friend's here. Sitting up on risers. Just hanging out, having a drink. I'm sitting up on the riser next to her, my new roommate. She's relaxed—she's got a drink—having a good time.

Her knee touches mine.

Her knee. My knee is frozen. I'm touching her. I don't pull away—or apologize. I let it happen—this knee-touching thing. This body-contact thing. It's natural. It just happened. It's the first time we've physically touched. It doesn't mean anything. She probably doesn't even notice that physically we're touching. And I can't hear the concert. I'm alone in the crowd—frozen—just me and her and my knee and her knee. Touching.

This is a major change in our relationship. *No, no, idiot—
your knee is brushed up against hers at a rock concert! Stupid,
stupid.* It doesn't mean anything. It's an accident. No—there
are *no* accidents. *Yes, yes, of course there are!* But it's still there.
She hasn't moved hers. Maybe she's too drunk to realize—
no . . . the knees . . . they're . . . they're just languishing there—

What does it all mean?

I call her *Bortai*. She calls me *Chimuga*. (Neither of us
can remember *Temujin*.)

I'm carrying a television down the street, to Soho. I
always seem to be carrying furniture down the street.
Manhattan is too small. No need for cars and vans and
pick-up trucks, much less hiring actual movers. So, I keep
carrying furniture back and forth, back and forth—from
here to her new apartment.

Her new apartment—it's smaller than the old one.
The one I still live in. It's about half the size, if you can
believe that, but it's a single—a one bedroom.

It's for the best. We agreed. The apartment was too small. Too small for two people who are involved in the kind of relationship we're involved in. Too close, too much, too soon. We both needed space, more space. We agreed. It's mutual. Of course, it is. Nothing is changing, really. We're going to have the same relationship. We're just not going to live together. It makes sense. Of course.

Nothing is changing.

It seems like we've already had the baby. He's been such a part of our lives now for eight-and-a-half months— especially the last three. We've taken every birthing and childcare class imaginable. I could probably teach a class on breast-feeding at this point, or maybe not. I knew tonight would be the night. I knew from the way she was pounding on the dummy at the CPR class earlier this eve-ning—that we would be here, now, doing this. Another surreal moment. Anxious. Exciting.

New apartment. Bigger. Transitional and in the sub-urbs. It's almost like a real home with a built-in dishwasher and usable garbage bins outside. Holy crap. Am I domestic?

I think one of the rocks over the fake fireplace looks like a bear's head.

Our picture taken on a beach.

Eating Mexican food.

I love the arcade. I'm way too old for this, but the little boy in me loves it. When I was a kid, it was all pinball machines and ski-ball and air hockey. Now, it's all video games. Actually, the ski-ball and air hockey are still here and even a couple of the pinball machines. So, really how much has changed? Credit the town for trading in on nostalgia, for realizing that folks want the fifties-era beachside resort community to remain a fifties-era beachside resort community while the planet's still spinning. It's certainly what I want.

I know she hates the arcade, but she smiles anyway, and I let her know she gets huge points for humoring me and catering to the whims of my inner eight-year-old. She's already humored my eight-year-old several times this trip. We ate breakfast at the restaurant with the giant taffy pulling machine in the window. We went to the newsstand and bought "Hot Stuff" and "Little Lotta" comics. As we play air hockey and pinball, I reflect that my inner eight-year-old has been pretty well taken care of.

I wonder what I can get at the prize booth for my forty Skee Ball points. There's not much you can get these days for forty points—but another ten and the rubber spider ring is mine. I see her standing in front of a funky-looking, ancient machine, definitely from the fifties—checking it out. She puts a buck in and tugs on this incredibly-difficult-to-pull stamper. The thing stamps out whatever you type onto a tiny metal Lucky Key Chain, embossed with horseshoes and four-leaf clovers. She stamps something out, knowing she can't go back and make changes. If she makes a mistake, it's set in there. It plops into the dispenser and she hands it to me:

BXRTQI LXUS CHMGA

I get her some water.

Soaked in sweat, hair matted.

I've spent months in classes, training to be her "coach"—but really, I don't do anything. I'm just there to be there. I say, "come on, honey" a lot. "You're doing great." "Come on." And I give her little chips of hard candy to suck on.

She's been carrying this medicine ball in her belly for months now. Through sheer force of will and physical exertion—and an excruciating, primal effort that will screw up her body for weeks to come—she will bring new life to the planet, for God sakes. Me, I'm going to hold little pieces of candy in a Dixie cup and try not to sound too idiotic.

"Push, honey. Push. Want some candy?"

In a pretty good tuxedo, I wait in front of a couple hundred of people all decked out in surprisingly nice formal wear. I have incredible gas. So, every cliché you hear is true. I didn't sleep the night before. I'm completely exhausted, but my beard looks great. Trimming my goatee is always an unpredictable experience. It's all guesswork.

Instinctive. The slightest jerk and the whole thing gets set-off. Unbalanced.

I'm going for short. She likes it short. However, today has to be special and much better than average. It has to have *flair*, almost a European salon look. And I have to do it myself—on no sleep, with the worst gas in history and a thousand things racing through my mind. No nicks. No bleeding. God forbid I cut slightly too much from one side. Then all that's left is to try to balance it—cut from the other side, cut from the first, balancing, balancing—till I've lost all perspective and then what? Nothing to do but shave the whole thing off, or cancel the wedding.

I'm surprisingly calm. Maybe it's lack of sleep. If anything, I'm giddy. But why not? Really, I don't have to do much. For once, showing up really is everything. Everyone looks so nice. I look nice. Hell, the whole thing is nice. I can enjoy this. It's just hard to take it all so seriously.

And then she appears.

This person I've known my whole life, now. This angel in white with that black, black hair walks towards me. *Me.* Her eyes sparkle. Her smile literally lights up the room. Everyone stares at her, breathless. And suddenly, she's there, beside me—and everything else ceases to exist. The family, the priest, the rabbi, my gas, my exhaustion, everything.

Yes, yes, the ceremony is lovely. But look at this. Suddenly, I *am* the luckiest son-of-a-bitch in town.

She learns how to play poker.
Better than me.

Jerry Garcia dies.

"Push, honey!"
"C'mon!"
"You can do it!"

We don't actually own the house yet. We own it as of tomorrow, but we've got the keys. For all intents and purposes, it's our house.

Our house.

We're ripping up the carpeting. God forbid the deal goes south in the next twelve hours as we would then be ripping up carpeting in someone else's house. However, it's unlikely the deal will go south. The carpet is funky, old, discolored, extremely lumpy in the middle. This is the master bedroom. What were these people thinking? Obviously, personal comfort wasn't very important to them.

Ripping up the carpet is invigorating. It's like a New Year—a new life. Out with the old and in with us. We paid for it. We paid the broker, the inspector, the lawyer. We trudged through snow and slush. We cut notices out of the paper and taped them to blank pages and made phone calls and argued and toured neighborhoods every time we saw an "open house" sign. We saw houses. A dozen, at least. And now we've bought one. Surely, we must be adults now. Right?

Look at us: gleeful, delinquent teens—the Bonnie and Clyde of carpet removal—sneaking into the old man's house while he's on vacation and ransacking his property, only there is no old man and it's our property. Or it will be tomorrow, anyway. We are primal, unprofessional in our carpet rippings, heaving and sweating.

Neither of us has ripped up carpet before. We knew something was holding it down. Nails? Tacks? Stapled, to the floor and to thin, brittle, wooden planks framing the carpet. As we rip and pull, millions of staples and nails jut out at us, everywhere.

How do people in houses dispose of things? Throw it on the street? Hope someone picks it up? Take it to a dump? We don't even know how our own garbage works. Where's a landlord when you need one?

I go out to find where the trash is kept. Three cans under an eave at the right side of the house, before the garage. Okay. Great. So, someone must pick it up.

"Garbage picks up Tuesday and Friday, but we have to call them to get service started back up."

"They discontinued service?"

The trash cans are full. Great. The sellers discontinued service and left us weeks-worth of rotting food and trash.

"Get rid of it! Get it out of here! Take the carpet with you!"

"Get rid of it?"

"Take it! It stinks! Go on!"

"Where?"

I load the garbage and carpet into my car trunk. Maggots crawling across the garbage bags drop into my trunk. The stench is unbearable. I drive back to our old apartment complex and dump everything in the trash bins. No one sees me. No one cares. Technically, I'm still a tenant till the end of the month. I heave the carpet with my super strength. The carpet is gone. Gone.

Over the course of the week, I make three more trips back to the complex before we determine how to get our garbage picked up.

We are proud new owners of a house.

We discover we like basketball.

Several doctors and nurses attend us—a lot of people for such an intimate experience. And then ... and then ... oh boy ... there he is ... really ... his head ... his eyes ... arms ... his legs ... his tiny tiny feet curled up. He's out. Out! There he is, Mrs. We—we actually have a baby.

And we're a family, suddenly. We must be adults, now. We must be. And the angel in white is lying on the bed, smiling and crying, exhausted, spent, resting, recovering.

Then, there—he's—he's in my arms. My son. My little boy. So small. Hardly anything. He's so small. He's beautiful. My boy. My little, little boy. Our boy.

Our son.

Translated: *Bortai loves Chimuga.*

Bits & Pieces

Random Thoughts

Tis better to have loved and lost than to be Lost in Space.

I was a late bloomer. Well actually, I was more of an exploder.

I once went out with a girl named Tanya, but her friends called her "Nya."

At the grocery today I saw some loose morels.

I never know what to do at parties. I'm always the guy in the corner smoking a beer.

What once were vices now are hobbies.

Wedding Pictures I've Ruined through Inappropriate Facial Hair

Shortly after college I was in my friend Dave's wedding party and I wore a massive, outlandish, unkempt beard which looked just awful on me. Of course, no one else in the wedding party had any facial hair whatsoever. So, now, in page after page of his wedding pictures, I stick out like a sore thumb. Did I consciously plan to ruin his wedding album? Who knows? However, I remember he had an extremely polite wedding party. *Oh, you look great! What a nice suit!* They were way too polite to ask this lunatic they barely knew to shave.

A Short High School Reunion Play

SALLY and DOUG see each other at their 10-year high school reunion. Sally, who used to be very shy, looks phenomenally successful and at the top of her field.

DOUG: Hey, Sally—what happened to you?!

SALLY: I started having sex, Doug!

DOUG: Wow! Sex did all that?!

SALLY: Sure did! Built up my self-confidence, gave me a real workout—and y'know what?! It's fun, too!

DOUG: Wow! Do you think sex could do all that for me?

SALLY: *(laughs)* Probably not everything, Doug! But it's a start!

Why Can't I Look in the Fridge?

Why does my significant other need to ask me what I'm looking for in the fridge? Why is that a thing? Why can't I just endlessly look in the goddamn fridge? *What are you looking for? Can I help you with something?* I'm looking for Seagram's Golden Wine Coolers. I'm looking for French Danishes. I'm looking for my dignity. Is it hiding behind the LaCroix seltzers? When did our fridge become precious and curated? *There's nothing in there you need to see. Now, close the door. The temperature's rising!*

My partner does not like it when I put shredded cheese on a sandwich. *It's just not right! Please don't do it!*

Brief Conversations On a Train

Him: I dreamed you cheated on me with one of my high school friends.

Her: I would never cheat on you with one of your high school friends. (*Attractive guy with cool socks and hipster douche beard walks by.*) With *him*, maybe.

Her: I'm pre-forgiving you.

Him: What does that mean?

Her: It means I assume you're going to be a complete
ass later, so I'm forgiving you now, ahead of
time.

Him: Okay. Could you go ahead and pre-forgive
me for the next five years?

Him: I don't need your undivided attention. Your
divided attention is just fine.

Her: You know where you don't want to go? *There.*
You don't want to go there.

Him: (*singing*) You say *tomato*. I say—well—since you said *tomato*, why don't we just go with *tomato*? No, no what I was going to say—no, don't worry about it. *Tomato* is fine. Sure, sure, that's great. Let's do that. Let's go with *tomato*.

The Qualified Apology

If you want to maintain a successful relationship, try not to use *The Qualified Apology*. *The Qualified Apology* is just like a regular apology—but with a *but . . .* added on at the end. And that *but . . .* negates the entire apology. For example, *I'm sorry . . . but you were an asshole.*

See, that first part—that *I'm sorry*—that's the perfect apology. Is it standard? Sure. But that's okay. It's simple. Effective. Sincere. *I'm sorry.* Period. Nothing else needed. But adding that *but . . .* well, now you've ruined the whole thing. That *but . . .* is a sure sign of someone who is not only *not* sorry—but who is by no means ready to disengage from the monumentally trivial thing that you've been fighting about for the past three hours. It's a way of saying *see, you thought it was time to make up, but I've gotten my wind back and I'm ready for Round Ten.*

There are many variations of *The Qualified Apology.* There's the classic version: I'm sorry, but ... you were *an idiot.* There's *The Qualified Apology with Clarification: I'm sorry, but ... you were an idiot. Had you NOT been an idiot— then I'd actually be sorry. But you were. So that's how the chips fell.* Another popular variation is *The Double-back Qualified Apology* where the Apologizer teeter-totters on the sincere apology before finally totally giving in to the regular *Qualified* version: *I'm sorry, but you were an idiot. But I am sorry. But you were an idiot. But ... I am sorry. But you know what? You were an idiot!!! I mean—what the hell am I sorry for?! I'm not sorry!!! You should be apologizing to me!! Jerk!*

Random Thoughts

Tis better to have loved and lost than to work in the Lost and Found department. Or the Complaints department, for that matter.

Celia and I kept in touch over the years: by phone, by email and finally just by yelling out the window.

I practice monogamy, and I like to practice it with as many people as possible.

I once got an email from a trusted impotence solution. Which is better than getting an email from a dubious impotence solution.

Absence makes the heart lose interest.

Advice Regarding Your Upcoming Marriage

Being married will prepare you for just about everything except germ warfare.

Consider establishing a marriage contract for three years with an option to renew.

Consider adding the marriage vow "*and do you solemnly swear to put up with each other's bullshit year after year after year?*"

And then, every year on your anniversary, you can toast each other and say, *thank you so much, darling, for continuing to put up with my bullshit.*

Things you will never hear in your lifetime: *Wow! You are SUCH a good driver! So smooth! Not too slow, not too fast! Just perfect! Bravo!*

More Wedding Pictures I've Ruined through Inappropriate Facial Hair

A few years after Dave's wedding, my Mom got remarried and asked me if I'd give her away at the ceremony.

"I'm ready to give," I said.

I glanced through the wedding pictures recently and, for some reason, I wore huge—I mean *huge*—mutton chops. Something I'd never worn before and haven't worn since. It's almost as if I had grown the things overnight simply to ruin her wedding.

I'm also a little surprised that my girlfriend, who wouldn't let me leave the apartment without changing shirts fifteen times, let me appear at the wedding with those monsters. To be fair, she'd just met my family. So, maybe she thought kooky hair and outfits were appropriate. Or maybe she knew it would be a good laugh years later when we looked at the album.

An Interfaith Wedding

My wife and I had an interfaith wedding. My parents were also interfaith as were all my grandparents. So, I come from a long line of religious ambivalence.

It's a real commitment being interfaith. Finding that fence, parking yourself on top of it and defending your goddamn right to stay there balancing smack dab in the middle. There's tremendous pressure to pick sides. But, to this day, we remain fanatically indecisive.

For the wedding, we knew we wanted a priest *and* a rabbi to perform the ceremony. And we considered throwing in two judges and a monkey just for good measure. The ceremony was held in a church and it was quite difficult to find a rabbi who would perform the ceremony there. We finally found an incredibly reformed rabbi on Craig's List. He said for two grand he would not only perform the service in a church, but if we wanted, he could do it on a unicycle juggling fire sticks. So, that was a great deal and at the service only a few missalettes caught fire.

Our Diet Adventure

My wife and I have been dieting together. And it's been great. But when you diet alongside a loved one you should determine right at the beginning if you have the same goals or if they diverge at some point. So, when we first started, my wife said her goal was to stay on the diet—*forever! Forever!!* She wanted to get back to her birth weight. And so, what was my plan? And I said, my plan was to drop a few and then get back to Taco Bell as fast as humanly possible. So, it's a good idea to know your *Diet Exit Strategy*.

We argue about the diet a little bit. She goes—*you should drink more water! I'm drinking eighteen gallons of water an hour!* And I say, *no, I'd rather drink eighteen gallons of Taco Bell hot sauce. But thank you.*

We've been doing it for a while, and it's been awesome because we discovered that we've both been mutually psychotic about almost everything we're doing. Like, we went to our favorite restaurant the other night—*Diet Date Night!*—and our favorite waiter said, *would you like your usual? The filet mignon drenched in butter?* And we said, *no, no—just bring us a small bowl of raspberries and eighteen gallons of water. Each.* And of course, our favorite waiter looks at us like—*eff you*—because the tip on a bowl of raspberries is much much less than on two filet mignons dripping in butter.

Then, after our meal—how do we end the perfect *Diet Date Night?* We go home and watch *The Food Network.* We watch Guy Fieri inhaling deep fried mac and cheese wrapped in pork rinds. And to set the mood, my wife lights one of her scented candles. And what's the scent? *Baked cookies!* Baked chocolate chip cookies. *Hey honey, how many calories is the candle?! Can we maybe just eat the candle?*

Random Thoughts

Tis better to have loved and lost than to do flood repair work in New Jersey.

I like to think I'm Woke, but I'm probably just *napping.*

My wife's heart is in the right place—on the left side of her chest—unlike mine which is down below my kidneys.

My wife and I discovered that whenever we get in a big fight, we immediately clean the house afterwards. So, now we try to get in a big fight at least once a month. We want to kill each other, but damn, you can eat off the floor.

If *Burger King* married *Dairy Queen* would they live at *White Castle*?

Don't Veer

My wife and I flew to Cincinnati for my nephew's bar mitzvah. We got in very late and by the time we got to the hotel the rent-a-car had completely broken down. So, my wife says *go back to the airport and get a new car*. It's around midnight and a forty-five minute trip back to the airport. But whatever. She stays at the hotel and I head back. But when I get to the rental car place, the replacement car they give me is new. Like *new* new. Like the newest car I've ever been in in my life. It's a 2021, Tesla/Prius super, triple-bypass hybrid that runs on electricity and liquid nitrogen and cocaine and tiger's blood and Altoids.

I get on the highway and the car has switches and dials and digital readouts—basically it's *Speed Racer's Mach 5*. And I'm trying to figure out how to pop out the buzz saws and the homing pigeon, when this incredibly sexy voice comes on and says, *my left rear tire could use just a little more air*. It's not flat—but it's not perfect. And the car wants to be *perfect*.

My car, I discover, is a bit of a diva. But I *love* this car—this sexy voice car. I'm essentially having an affair with my car—and I want to make the car happy. I'm not even driving back to the hotel—I've just been circling the airport for fifteen minutes. So, I find an all-night gas station with an air hose and I fill the tire and the car likes that. *I like that. Thank you. That's . . . nice. Please continue driving.* And I get back on the road.

And after a minute the voice comes back on—*you're veering slightly to the left. Please correct your alignment. Don't veer. Please don't veer.* On the dashboard there's a stick figure picture of the highway with a line running down it, and the car is slightly to the left of the line. I feel like I'm Luke Skywalker unsuccessfully trying to stay in the *Death Star trench.*

And I realize I can't *not* veer. At this point, my entire life is about slightly veering one way or the other—and that's not going to change in the middle of the night, when I'm already exhausted. *Don't veer. Please correct your alignment.*

I realize my sexy new car is *not* the *Mach 5.* The car has become my second wife. And now I have to pull over and figure out how to turn all this helpfulness off before my *real* wife gets in the car—because if my real wife gets in the car, then she and the car will double-team me.

Car: *Don't veer!*

Wife: *See, that's what I said! You're veering and you're being defensive!*

So, I pull over onto the shoulder and start looking for the kill switch. Because the rental car guy said there was a switch that would turn the voice off. But on the other hand, this was a guy whose necktie only came halfway down his shirt, so who knows how reliable he was.

So, I'm looking for the switch and suddenly the car becomes suspicious. *What are you doing? There's nothing wrong with the car.* And suddenly, I'm in the movie *2001, A Space Odyssey. There's nothing wrong with the car. Nothing under the dashboard. Please get back on the road.*

But I find the switch and I hit it. *What—what are you—what are you—Daisy, Daisy . . .* And my super-advanced, sexy car becomes just another regular boring car. I'm so relieved, and I pull back onto the highway just barely sideswiping an airport shuttle. I get all the way back to the hotel and park the car in the lot. I get into the high-tech hotel elevator and the doors shut. The elevator goes up half a floor and lurches to a stop.

And a sexy mechanical elevator voice says
I know what you did.

In Closing

Good night. Get some rest.
Don't forget to turn off the lights.

About the Author

Alex Bernstein is the award-winning author of *Miserable Adventure Stories* and *Plrknib*. His work has appeared at *McSweeney's*, *NewPopLit*, *The Big Jewel*, *The American Bystander*, *Gi60*, *Yankee Pot Roast*, *Swink*, *Litro*, *Back Hair Advocate*, *Corvus*, *BluePrintReview*, *Hobo Pancakes*, *The Rumpus*, *The Legendary*, *MonkeyBicycle*, and *PopImage*, among numerous others. Please visit him at www.promonmars.com.